Jeff A Big Ed Wood Fan!

DARK CITIES:

Dark Tales

Don't Be Afraid, of the Dark!

MICHAEL McCARTY

DARK CITIES: DARK TALES

Michael McCarty

This is a work of fiction. Names, characters, locations and events depicted in this book are products of the author's imagination or are -- not, or and used fictitiously. Any resemblance to actual persons, living or dead or actual events is purely coincidental.

Printed in the United States of America.

ISBN: 9781688422612

Editor: Ann Attwood
Proofreaders: Cindy McCarty, Bradley Heden, Holly Zaldivar, Connie Sherwood,
*   Sarah Holderfield & Jeff Ernst*
Layout & Design of the book: Sarah Holderfield

ALSO BY MICHAEL McCARTY:

Short Story Collections:

Dark Duets by Michael McCarty (2005) Wildside Press
A Little From My Fiends by Michael McCarty (2014) Wildside Press
Dracula Transformed & Other Bloodthirst Tales by Mark McLaughlin &
Michael McCarty (2016) Wildside Press
Dark Cities: Dark Tales by Michael McCarty (2019) Amazon

Novels:

Apocalypse America! by Michael McCarty & Mark McLaughlin (2019) Amazon
Liquid Diet & Midnight Snack by Michael McCarty (2011) Simon & Schuster
Bloodless series: Bloodless, Bloodlust & Bloodline by Michael McCarty & Jody
LaGreca (2012), (2013), (2016)

Novellas:

Lost Girl Of The Lake by Joe McKinney & Michael McCarty (2017)
Grinning Skull Press
I Kissed A Ghoul by Michael McCarty (2015) Curiosity Quills Press

Non-Fiction:

Modern Mythmakers by Michael McCarty (2013) Crystal Lake Press
Conversations with Kreskin by The Amazing Kreskin & Michael McCarty
(2012) Team Kreskin
Ghosts of the Quad Cities by Michael McCarty & Mark McLaughlin (2019)
Haunted America

TABLE OF CONTENTS:

1   *Strangelove by Michael McCarty*

99   *The Sludge by Michael McCarty & Mark McLaughlin*

111   *Red Snow by Michael McCarty*

117   *Terror of Bristol Plains by Joe McKinney & Michael McCarty*

167   *The Stone Bridge Trolls by Michael McCarty*

171   *The Collective by C.L. Sherwood and Michael McCarty*

181   *Alone With A Demon by Michael McCarty*

200   *About The Authors*

ACKNOWLEDGMENTS: Wildside Press, Grinning Skull Press, Don D'Ammassa, Igor's Bistro, Steve McCarty and family, The Hultings, The Leonards, Holly Olsen, Janet Clark, Quinn, Joan Mauch, Linnea Quigley, Amber, Char, Camilla, The Amazing Kreskin, Cheri Brink, Linda Cook, Christopher & Valerie Miron, John Huff, Bonnie Lou, Todd Boyer, Debra Winter, the memory of Kitty The Bunny, *The Quad City Times, Midnite Mausoleum, Acri Creature Feature, Svengoolie, Zomboo, Rue Morgue* magazine, Burlington By The Book, Ann Attwood Editing & Proofreading Services and Sarah Holderfield.

And The Cities:

"Strangelove" - Angel Falls, Florida, Daytona Beach, Florida, Okefenokee Swamp, Florida, Chattanooga, Tennessee, Indianapolis, Indiana, Chicago, Illinois and Davenport, Iowa and the Quad Cities
"The Sludge" – New York, New York
"Red Snow" – Rock Island, Illinois
"The Terror of Bristol Plains" – Bristol Plains, Texas
"The Stone Bridge Trolls" – Waukegan, Illinois
"The Collective" – Eerie, Indiana
"Alone With A Demon" – Hades, Texas and Davenport, Iowa

FOR MY PARENTS:

GERALD D. MCCARTY
June 18, 1939 – November 15, 2007

BEVERLY J. MCCARTY
February 28, 1942 – October 16, 2017

TO MY LOVELY WIFE:

Cindy McCarty: Who brightens the darkest of cities.

TO OLD FRIENDS:

Mark McLaughlin
Ron Stewart
Raymond Congrove
Brad Heden
William Curtis Mohr

Joe McKinney
Mel Piff
David & Julie Thompson
The Source Book Store
And the memory of Scott Madsen

AND TO NEW FRIENDS:

Holly Zaldivar
Latte The Bunny
Jo Ann Brown
Connie Sherwood
Chef Steph
Brian Kronfeld

Jeff Ernst
Bruce Cook
Marlena Midnite
The Book Rack
And the memory of Lyle Ernst

I've written five vampire novels and one vampire short story collection. I've decided to write a vampire novella. I also wanted to write a story about the publishing business that can be "bloodthirsty" at times. I combined the two ideas and came up with this. The title is a Depeche Mode song. I also owe a huge thanks to Bradley Heden, Holly Zaldivar, Connie Sherwood, Cindy McCarty, Sarah Holderfield & Jeff Ernst for their assistance with this tale…

STRANGELOVE
by Michael McCarty

"Better to reign in Hell, than serve in Heav'n" – *Paradise Lost* by John Milton
"The blood is the life!" – *Dracula* by Bram Stoker

All bad things come to an end. We aren't going to start at the end of the story, though, but at the beginning –

This story actually begins right here, right now, in Angel Falls, a once bustling tourist town with the famous Sea Slide Amusement Park in Florida. The theme park, long ago shut down, still stands like a ghost town with rides. The big revenue maker for the town is Angel Falls University, an overpriced private college.

With summer just around the corner, Angel Falls University will end another school year and half the population will leave for about two and a half months, but will re-start again in the late summer, early fall. Summer hasn't arrived yet; AFU still has a couple more weeks, holding onto the last few days like an old man in the middle of the ocean with a worn out life preserver.

Outside it's a hot, humid, and hazy Florida evening, but we aren't concerned about the weather, because we're at a lecture in an auditorium that has air conditioning. Not many are attending this discourse about writing – mostly English students trying to get extra credit, some of the faculty and staff obligated to come to these events, a few budding writers, and even fewer from the general public. The hall is reasonably quiet except – for the occasional cough or scrape of a folding chair across linoleum.

1

CHAPTER ONE:

STRANGER IN A STRANGE LAND
Angel Falls University
Angel Falls, Florida

With her cat-like eyes blazing over the audience, Corrie Mohr-Wright checked the microphone and leaned forward on the podium. "Alfred Hitchcock understood character development."

The audience clapped.

"Yes, the Master of Suspense really knew how to do it. We have the retired San Francisco detective John 'Scottie' Ferguson who suffered from acrophobia in *Vertigo*. The icy blonde socialite Melanie Daniels who always got what she wanted in *The Birds*. And of course, too handsome for his own good, government agent T.R. Devlin in *Notorious*."

She paused, stood straight, and flipped a shock of wavy, auburn hair from her eyes. Again, she leaned, lips almost touching the microphone, hand flat on the podium. "And perhaps one of the best examples, distillations of character development can be found in his example of the MacGuffin. Every character, every well written character, has a MacGuffin, if it is to be a believable character." She relaxed a bit, took a sip of water, and set the glass back down on the table beside the podium with an audible click. "A character's MacGuffin is what he or she wants most in the world. It's what makes each of them get out of bed in the morning."

The auditorium was silent.

"And here is the tough part," she continued. "As writers, more often than not you will need to learn to work without a net. Sometimes a character's motivations aren't known to an author until a substantial amount of writing has been done. Remember: the characters are the ones telling the story; all the writer has to do is get it down on paper."

She pointed to a raised hand near the front row – a young woman in a light gray dress stood.

"So, are you saying that an author doesn't need to know a character's motivations and that the character will reveal it them during the writing process?"

"That isn't what I said at all," Corrie snapped. "You would think with the amount of money each of you paid to be here, you would pay more attention."

Nervous laughter and a shuffling of feet; the girl in the gray dress turned scarlet.

"What I said is that sometimes a character's MacGuffin is not obvious to a writer at the beginning of a novel, and that when the plot is moving forward successfully, of its own impetus, a character's goals will often become clear. Sometimes these motives change. Sometimes they are not what the author wanted or had anticipated. A character in a novel is an actor, and an actor must act, not merely be acted upon by forces around him or her. And most importantly of all, sometimes a character doesn't want what the writer wants them to want, but that is all part of the creative process – the courage to allow your characters to take the story where it will."

Glancing at a large wall clock at the back of the auditorium she smiled and said, "And that, for me, is it for this evening, thank God."

Professor Suzanne Morgan hobbled across the stage with her wooden cane. She picked up the microphone. "Thank you, Corrie Mohr-Wright. As many of you know, she is a former student here, in fact, one of *my* students. She will be selling and signing copies of her Granny Smith books, including her latest, at the table near the back."

Corrie sat at the table with her stacks of hardcover and paperback books. Most of the audience filed past her; some murmured encouraging comments. Only one student bought a paperback. In her late forties, she made it a point to dress as young and professional as possible. She wore a designer black dress meant for that purpose, but it only served to show off her voluptuous figure.

A tall, young man escorted Professor Morgan to the table.

"How much is your latest book?" Professor Morgan asked.

"*Penny Dreadful.* Twenty five dollars, but I can't charge you –"

"Don't be ridiculous. I'm over compensated for my services at the university." She smiled as she handed Corrie a fifty-dollar bill.

"I'll get you some change –"

"No I want two copies. One for myself, of course. And the other for a former student, Ian Strange, he is also a promising writer."

"Ian Strange? Is that a pen name?"

"Nope, not at all." A tall, lanky, young man stepped forward. He had piercing dark eyes and thick, chestnut brown hair, a goatee, and a devious smile that could only lead to trouble. "Real name. I come from the Strange family, or should I say, my family has always been strange. By the way, I'm the assistant manager of the C-Store at the university." He held out his hand which Corrie shook.

"I'm used to meeting strange people all the time. Occupational hazard."

Ian's smile brightened. "Your author photo doesn't do you justice."

"Flattery will get you everywhere, young man," she replied with a quick laugh. Corrie opened the first book, penned an inscription and handed it back to the elderly professor. She did the same thing to the second book and handed it to Mr. Strange.

"Thanks. Would you mind signing another?" He pulled out a trade paperback and handed it to her.

"Sure." She looked down at the cover. "*Dark Wave.* That book has to be even older than you are, Mr. Strange."

"Ian. Please call me Ian."

"Okay, Ian."

"Not quite. That book is twenty years old. I'm twenty-six."

Corrie smiled, signed the book and gave it back to him.

"Corrie, Ian," Professor Morgan said, "It is getting late for me. I've got to get home and feed my cats. Nice seeing you again, Corrie."

Once the professor was across the room, Ian said, "I really enjoyed your lecture. I'm a big fan of Hitchcock, especially *Psycho.*"

"I thought your generation had given up on Hitchcock. *Psycho* is rather tame compared to all the *Saw* and *Friday the 13th* movies. "

"Much of the *Psycho* movie's plot is skillfully foreshadowed by clever, ironic passages of dialogue. Norman's comment that 'a boy's friend is his mother,' is ironic, because his mother is dead and still lives on as one of his split-personalities," Ian explained.

"You are a big fan."

"Norman's mother is also very birdlike: she's stuffed, like one of Norman's winged taxidermy projects. Norman mentions birds are so non-aggressive. Really? What about eagles, owls, falcons, ravens and vultures? Even chickens peck at each other, and Norman's mother certainly pecks without mercy at him. I'm sorry, I get carried away sometimes."

"Very insightful," Corrie said. "Did you study film here at the college?"

"Nope, I was a Poli-Sci major with a minor in English. Do you need any help hauling back all those books?"

She glanced at the stack of books on the edge of the table and sighed, "The college will send someone along to take care of them."

"I was hoping I could walk you back to your car so we could talk. I'm an author myself and have written a book," Ian admitted.

Corrie rolled her eyes. "I'm not an editor or an agent. If I had a dollar for every author who hit me up to read a book, I wouldn't need to sell mine anymore." She opened her purse and pulled out a flier. "There is a writers' conference next weekend in Daytona Beach. I have a lecture and a signing. Maybe you can make some connections."

"Thanks. I'll probably be seeing you there."

CHAPTER TWO:

STRANGE NAME
Daytona Beach Writers Conference
Pirate's Treasure Chest Hotel

Ian tossed his plastic keycard on the bed and grabbed the ringing telephone. "Hello?"

"Ian?" Elaine asked. "I've been calling all evening. Where were you?"

"Attending a lecture," he said. "You didn't think I was going to spend my time sitting in my room?"

"I tried to reach you on your cell but it was turned off."

"Honey, it was a lecture. You are supposed to turn your cell phone off."

Elaine sighed, "I was just worried about you. That's all."

"It's alright. I was going to call you as soon as I got back to the room."

"So are you learning anything?" she asked.

He drew the curtains aside and looked down toward the street where the road ended at the beach. Palm trees swayed in the ocean breeze and he tasted the salt on his lips. The moonlight glistened on his skin. He'd have to enjoy this weather while it lasted; hurricane season was two months away.

"Some of the seminars have been interesting; others not so much."

"Have you made any useful connections? Have you been networking? Giving out those overpriced business cards?" she asked.

"Not yet, but this is only day one. Still have tomorrow."

"Did you meet any interesting writers?" Elaine continued. "Anyone who might be able to help you get your book published?"

"Uh, I did meet someone who said they might be interested in reading *Ask Twice*."

"What is his name?"

"Corrie Mohr-Wright."

"Who did you say?"

He let the curtain fall and sat on the edge of the bed.

"Maury. Maury Cartright."

"He sounds like a shoe salesman. Are you sure you can trust him?"

"As far as you can trust anyone in the publishing business," he laughed. "You know what they say. Publish or perish."

"Did he say he would publish your book?"

"Not exactly."

"Well, did he say he would read it?"

"Not really," Ian responded.

"Not really? He said he wouldn't read it?"

"I haven't gotten around to asking him yet," he admitted. "We're meeting for drinks later tonight. He has a redeye flight back to Miami."

"What does he look like?" Elaine asked.

"He's, fair, average looking, rather anonymous – couldn't pick him out of a police lineup."

"I picture a man in a porkpie hat and suspenders, with a napkin tucked in his shirt, eating a coleslaw and brisket sandwich."

"That's Maury –"

"I will Google him and see if he's legit," she said. "You can't be too careful of anyone these days."

"No need to do that," Ian said quickly. "I'm sure he's on the up and up."

"Well, I'm going to."

"He writes under a pen name. A pseudonym. You wouldn't be able to find out anything about him online."

"Well what is his pen name? His pseudonym?"

"Elaine, if I knew his pen name it wouldn't be a pseudonym. You are being silly. Don't worry about it."

"What? That doesn't make any sense. Ian, what's wrong?"

"Look, the maid is here," he rushed to end the conversation. "Have to run. I will call you later and let you know how it went."

Ian hung up the phone, closed the window, lay down on the mattress and stared at the stucco ceiling.

He closed his eyes enjoying the silence. By his feet was his briefcase with *Ask Twice*, the book he'd begun working on when he started college, but didn't complete until a year after he graduated. At eighty thousand words it felt like he wrote over eight million.

CHAPTER THREE:

STRANGERS IN THE NIGHT
The Booty Bar and Grill
Pirate's Treasure Chest Hotel
Daytona Beach, Florida

"Enter the third murderer," Corrie quipped as Ian slid into the opposite side of the booth, laying a thick spiral notebook on the edge of the table. She sipped her Scotch and leaned back against the upholstered leather, closing her eyes.

"What was that?" he inquired.

She repeated, "Enter the third murderer."

"Should I know that? The reference."

"You would if you knew your Shakespeare as well as you do your Hitchcock."

"*MacBeth*," he grinned.

"Bingo."

Ian ordered a gin and tonic, then turned to Corrie who was watching him with a thin smile.

"That was John Cheever's drink," she said. "Gin and tonic."

"I didn't know that," he admitted.

"Noel Coward's as well."

"Are the drinking preferences of famous writers a hobby of yours?"

"No," she smiled. "Only my own drinking habits are a hobby of mine."

His drink arrived and with visible disdain, he removed the small plastic sword from the wedge of lime, placing it on the table.

"As hotel bars go, this one isn't too bad," he noted. He looked at the rows of hardcover books in the shelves above her head, all of them classics, but probably bought by the yard. There was even an upright piano to the left of the bar, the keys covered with a black velvet runner.

"Carpe librum," Corrie offered with a smile.

"You mean Carpe diem?" he asked, confused.

"No. Carpe librum is Latin for 'seize the book.' Carpe diem is 'seize the day.' I meant to say, 'seize the book.'"

Ian nodded, then pointed to the books above her head, "Whoever decorated has good taste in books. *East Of Eden, To Kill A Mockingbird, Atlas Shrugged, The Beautiful And Damned, To Have and Have Not.* Is that why you come here? Because of the books?"

"I came here for the Scotch," she confided. "And here I have no reason to worry that I might be recognized."

"Recognized?"

"Among the classics. No one would expect to find me here nestled in among the classics. My books are on bookshelves or at libraries, and occasionally, I bet they are being used as doorstops, but I shudder to think of that."

"You had a decent enough turnout this evening," he reassured her. "At your lecture."

"And what did you think of it? My lecture?"

"I thought it was an excellent summary of outlining versus, not outlining a story or a book."

Corrie smiled and sipped her Scotch. The ice tinkled in the glass. She licked her lips, enjoying, savoring the taste of the imported whisky. She idly ran her fingertip around the rim. "I see we are having a threesome," nodding toward the notebook.

"What?"

"I see you brought your child."

"Oh, yeah," he confessed. "I was wondering if you would consider —"

"You were wondering if I would have a look at your MacGuffin?"

He bowed his head for a moment, knowing she must be bombarded by such requests. Clearing his throat, he finally said, "Well, yes."

"Your breakout novel?"

Ian ran his hands through his hair and sighed, glancing at his watch. He signaled the waiter and ordered another Scotch.

"As long as we are doing this, let's do it right. Give me your pitch."

"My what?"

"Your pitch. Tell me what your book is about in fifty words or less."

"Well, it's kind of hard to put into just a few words. It's an eighty thousand word book."

"Do you know what it's about?"

"Well, of course I know what it's about," he said too fast. "I wrote it. How could I not know what it is about?"

"So tell me. Hook me. Pique my interest."

She watched him struggling for something to say and smiled, leaning forward and laying a hand on his shoulder. "Come here," she murmured.

"What?"

"Lean forward. I want to check something."

He leaned across the table and Corrie moved her hand from his shoulder to run her finger behind his ear.

"Yep. Just as I thought."

"What?"

"Still wet behind the ears."

He sighed again and looked at his watch.

"If you don't have time to read it, I understand. You have people asking you to read their manuscripts all the time. I don't know what I was thinking."

He started to rise, but she put her hand on his shoulder again.

"Don't give up so easily," she explained. "I never do. Not a good trait for a writer. I thought we were going to do this right."

Ian looked at the book and laid a hand on it as if he could break it. He took one last deep breath.

"*Ask Twice* is the story of a spy named Preston Whitehouse, who goes on vacation in the Caribbean. The problem, is that he doesn't know how to relax because of his profession. Every time Preston tries to kick back, get some sun, and have some fun, someone ends up dead."

"Interesting. Different. But I don't get the title"

"It is from a Danish proverb, 'Better to ask twice than lose your way once.'"

"Not too bad," she admitted interested. "But you need to polish your delivery a bit. Try to sound a little more confident."

"Alright."

"Now, let me ask you something," she continued. "If I don't like it, if I tell you it stinks, and believe me, if it stinks, I will tell you, could you handle that?"

"I suppose so."

"Good. That is a necessary part of the process, you understand. Part of our self-development, something we need to acknowledge as part of the writing process. Knowing that we sometimes write crap is always a difficult aspect for new writers to accept."

"I bet you have never written anything crappy in your life."

"Now you are just being foolish," she paused. "Have you ever made spaghetti?"

"Yes. All the time."

"The best way to make spaghetti is this: you fill the saucepan with a lot of sauce and you simmer it for an hour or two. You are actually simmering it down, down and down. And what you are left with is delicious. That is the same with writing. You simmer the novel down to the delicious stuff."

"I like that analogy."

She scooted a little closer to him. "What is she like?"

"Who like?"

"Your wife."

"How did you know I was married?" he said, lowering his eyes.

"It's written all over your face. It's in the way you keep checking your watch. The difficulty you have maintaining eye contact. The bulge of the ring in your left pocket. The best writers are observers; you pick up on the little things. How long have you been married?"

"Four years."

"I have you beat by eighteen. High school sweethearts?"

"No, we met in college. I really don't feel comfortable talking about my personal life."

"Look sweetie," she leaned in closer. "This is a partnership. We are in this together. I can see you're a little nervous. Maybe we should go back to my room for more privacy."

"Do you think that's a good idea?" he said. "I mean we're both married."

"If you're worried about looks, I'll go first and you can meet me there in about five minutes. I'm in room 313. Here's my extra keycard."

Before he could make a rebuttal, she was gone, like a freight train rolling down the tracks in the night.

CHAPTER FOUR:

STRANGE BEDFELLOWS
Pirate's Treasure Chest Hotel
Daytona Beach, Florida

Ian stood outside 313 with the briefcase in his hand. He felt weird about just barging in, although he did have the keycard. But on the other hand, he felt weirder about knocking. He slid in the card and opened the door.

Corrie's room was a spacious suite with gothic looking floor-to-ceiling windows and decorated with a king size bed, mini-bar, glass partition, enormous L-shaped couch, armchair, coffee table and a large desk with a laptop, notebooks and piles of crumpled papers. But she was nowhere to be seen.

"I'm in the bathroom," she shouted. "Make yourself comfortable. I'll be out in a couple of minutes."

Ian put his briefcase beside the bed and sat on the edge.

She stepped out of the bathroom wearing only a skimpy black slip that barely covered her black bra and matching panties. She, too, sat on the edge of the bed.

"You want me to get my hands on your manuscript and I want to get my hands on you," Corrie crooned in a husky soft voice. "I think you know what I want." She stared at him, transfixed, not taking her eyes off of him for a minute, like a lioness ready to pounce on its prey.

Ian knelt in front of her and took her two feet in his hands. He buried his face in her lap and then between her open legs. With one smooth movement her panties slid off.

She gripped the nape of his neck and brought him even closer, feeling his face pressing her inner thighs, feeling the heat from his face, the wetness of his tongue going inside of her.

Ian rubbed his cheek against her belly, then against her thighs, her inner things, and between her legs again and again.

Corrie was adrift in a sea of ecstasy, wave after wave of pleasure. She didn't remember taking off her slip or bra, or even Ian undressing, but she was lying on her stomach and he was on top of her, entering from behind. He caressed her breasts and thrust between her legs.

"That's good," she purred like a satisfied kitten. "Mama needs just a little more sugar."

He thrust even faster, panting like a dog in heat.

"Yes, that's it," she moaned. "Just a little more, baby. A little more —"

He grunted and rolled off of her.

She kissed him on the cheek and headed for the shower.

When Corrie came out of the bathroom again towel-less with a bottle of lotion, Ian was sleeping. She picked up the manuscript and took a seat on the sofa. By the soft light of the lamp, she began to read.

CHAPTER FIVE:

STRANGE DREAM
Pirate's Treasure Chest Hotel
Daytona Beach, Florida

Corrie wanted to hate the manuscript. Figuring she got laid, she thought she could brush him off by saying, "Sorry, kid. This needs work." But she was surprised. The work was good. Almost too good. A lot better than her first book *Dark Wave*. Her books didn't start getting this good until *Sweet Kiss Of Darkness*. It wasn't until her stomach grumbled that she finally put the papers down and walked over to the bed. Her eyes changed from green to gray. Softly she lifted up Ian's left wrist and gently sank her fangs into his tender flesh. Blood started flowing from the open wound. She drank and drank and drank until her hunger was satisfied. She put his wrist back on the bed and went back to reading.

While Corrie read the manuscript through the night, Ian visited dreamland with an unusually sensual and vivid dream.

On this warm summer night Ian and Corrie were on the widow's walk railed rooftop of a lighthouse. He knew the lighthouse – it had been abandoned for over a decade, but now it was lit, and a bright beam of blue light shone over the dark ocean. Her nimble fingers unbuttoned his shirt, one button at time, teasing, pleasing in the anticipation of things to come.

He caressed her face, which started to peel like it was sunburned and then it shed as a snake sheds its old skin until her face was laid bare, revealing the metal plate beneath. Her eyes were no longer green, but glowed red like dying embers on a campfire before the dawn.

Ian reeled when he saw Corrie's real face.

"Don't worry, love," she whispered as she began to peel his face; it shed just like hers until it was a mere steel plate with the same mechanical red eyes.

"We're the same, you know. Always have been, always will be," she softly kissed his metal face, but it was without passion, because she no longer had any lips.

CHAPTER SIX:

STRANGE AND STRANGER
Pirate's Treasure Chest Hotel
Daytona Beach, Florida

"Wake up loverboy," Corrie said, standing above Ian. She was dressed in a red designer dress and carried a briefcase in her hands. "I have to leave to catch my flight. I am taking your manuscript with me. I read the entire story and it shows promise."

"Really?" he said, trying to sound enthused, but was too tired. He rubbed the sleep out of his eyes, brushed the hair off of his face, yawned twice and finally sat up. "What time is it?"

"Eight."

"Eight o'clock in the morning?"

"No, eight o'clock at night."

"I slept for over twelve-four hours. How is that possible?"

"I wore you out," she explained with a wink. "Can't make any promises. I will show it to my agent Curtis Ballinger. That's why I am heading down to Miami. He's trying to make a book deal for my latest book, called *Kill Fee*."

"Fantastic!"

"I have some advice, but it is probably before your time."

"Try me."

"Have you heard of the band, The Wallflowers?"

"Yes, I play their song 'Sleepwalker,' on my iPod all the time."

"This is a slightly older song, 'One Headlight.'"

"Yes," Ian said, lifting his head above the pillow. "I know that one, too."

"That song seems to sum up the publishing industry all too well. It speaks to me, as an author, saying: 'You are driving in the dark night with only one headlight to guide you; trying to return to your house, with only partial vision to find your murky destination. Having some blind faith and a lot of luck, you might not crash the automobile and make it home alive.' Drive the best you can with the limited resources this business gives you."

Ian let the words sink in. "Corrie, I can't thank you enough. I really appreciate anything you can do for me. Can I ask you something?"

"Sure. Make it quick. Don't have much time."

"What is a kill fee?"

She laughed. "A kill fee is a fee that ensures the writers get paid for all the work they have done, but the publisher pays them only a fraction of what the book or magazine article would have originally paid. It is a clause in the contract. You'll have to read the book to discover the rest. I have your extra key and will check out shortly. Just shut the door when you leave."

Ian sat up. "Okay. I don't know how I can ever thank you, Corrie."

"Not to worry. Your tongue already did," she teased, exiting the room.

CHAPTER SEVEN:

STRANGE COURSE OF EVENTS
Six months later
The Cove Bar & Restaurant
Angel Falls, Florida

Curtis Ballinger booked a private conference room at the hotel between the dining room and the ballroom because it offered privacy, even if at a steep price. The small boxy room consisted of a black leather sofa and a glass coffee table with a bottle of tequila and two shot glasses. Of course it was all on Corrie's dime, including the booze and even the tip. He was tall and the ceiling was short. He ducked under the slow motion of the ceiling fan and didn't bump his bald head once. The room was private, so he couldn't complain too much. He adjusted the collar on his white suit and glanced down to be sure nothing had marked the jacket or pants.

Curtis stood on the darker side of the big table, away from the picture windows, adjusting his sunglasses when Corrie walked in; she was fifteen minutes late, but she was always late. Her cleavage-baring black blouse with a short tight black leather miniskirt and black sunglasses took his breath away, though he'd never let on to that effect.

"Just flew in from Miami and it was a turbulent flight all the way. Just the way my luck has been going lately," she said.

He nodded his head and softly said, "And I'm glad to see you, too, Corrie."

His remark made her smile.

"You might want a drink first." He poured two fingers of tequila and handed the glass to her. She smelled the aroma, then swallowed it down with a few seductive gulps.

"Another?"

"Is the news bad?" Corrie asked.

"Bad."

"How bad?"

"You might want another drink first, then I'll explain."

Corrie downed another double.

"Norton & MacKenzie Inc. turned down *Kill Fee*."

"What!"

"Please calm down."

"How is that possible? They published the other ten Granny Smith books."

"It is possible and nothing is certain in the publishing business." He poured two shots, handing her back her shot glass before downing his. "And it gets much worse. They want to discontinue the series. *Penny Dreadful* will be the last book."

"What?" She was stunned for a moment, only a moment, then snapped, "Goddamn it!" She paused. "Why?"

"There is an old saying in the book biz, you are only as good as your last book. They don't mean writing-wise, they mean sales-wise. The first five sold great, the last five not so great."

She was too numb to respond.

"A lot of bookstores have closed over the last couple of years and you sold a lot of your books at signings. It is all Amazon's fault, really," he said, taking another drink.

"I don't give a crap about Amazon. Could we get *Kill Fee* published from another publisher?"

"Nope. Norton & MacKenzie Inc owns the rights to the Granny Smith character."

"Goddamn it," Corrie fumed, trying to keep her emotions in check, but they went checkmate. "I spent six months writing that outline and another two months writing the first three chapters. Now the novel has just vaporized like a drizzle in a hot pan."

"You're very talented. You just need to believe that too," Curtis paused. "This is just a minor setback. Corrie, you'll bounce back on your feet in no time."

"For young writers it's a setback. Writers my age, it's a career killer."

Curtis placed another shot glass to his lips, paused to ponder, then took a drink. "There is a silver lining in this thunderstorm."

"What's that," she asked in a menacing monotone.

"Norton & MacKenzie likes your writing style and is open to looking at another book – as long as it isn't a Granny Smith book."

"That's a small comfort. I've spent a decade developing the character and series, and now it's gone to the big book recycler in the sky. My vibe has been killed. Maybe I can get it back with more tequila," Corrie said.

They both downed another shot

"Do you want to hear my advice?"

She didn't respond, just sighed. Finally she broke the silence. "Yeah. Sure. I guess. Why the hell not?"

"Take a year or two off. Write another fabulous book." He put his hand strategically on her knee.

She took his hand off her knee and crossed her legs.

"Come on Corrie," he spoke softly. "You don't have to take it out on me. I'm just the messenger. I'm still your agent. How long have I been your agent now?"

"For over ten years."

"Exactly. I've been looking out for your interests for a decade, making sure you got every dime of your royalties and the best advances possible, and even helped you with the book tours. I even paid for the airfare and hotel room in Dallas so you could attend that mystery writers' conference a couple of years ago. I did this for you, because I think you are a great writer. I still have a lot of faith in you."

She didn't say a word. She kept her head down.

He scooted closer to her, and put his hand back on her knee, sliding it upwards.

"So are they killing Ian Strange's book too?" she asked.

"Huh? What?"

"*Ask Twice.*"

"Corrie, you know I'm not allowed to divulge information about other clients or their books."

She removed his hand from between her legs. "You know, I am the one who discovered him. And brought you the manuscript. The easiest fifteen percent you ever made. You owe me!"

"Okay. You can't tell a soul." He slid closer to her, putting his hand back on her inner thigh "No, *Ask Twice* is going to get published by Norton & MacKenzie. The publisher thinks it's going to be a runaway hit."

"Goddamn, I knew it!"

"Shhhhh!" He moved his finger to his lips, then moved his hand between her legs again. "It gets much worse. They are giving Mr. Strange a big advance. Besides the lackluster sales they were planning on eventually letting you go anyway. But the timing was right for them."

She didn't say a word, just simmered like a pot of chili.

"I got them to keep you on the roster for another novel or series. I'm putting my ass on the line for you. Look on the bright side —"

"I tried but it hurt my eyes."

"When life throws you lemons —"

"You duck so they can hit the guy behind you." She paused. "I'm having so much goddamn bad luck."

Curtis scooted closer to her and whispered in her ear. "The good thing with luck is this: it can always turn around."

She buried her head in his shoulder and didn't say a word.

They were both silent

Finally, the agent broke the silence. "You can still be nice to me?" He moved his hand up her thigh again for good measure.

She didn't answer.

"Do you want to go back to my room?" he continued.

"No, not your room, it isn't going to be that long anyway. Do you have a car rental?"

"Yes. A black minivan."

"On what level of the parking garage?"

"Fifth."

"Pay the bill and I will meet you at your minivan in fifteen minutes."

CHAPTER EIGHT:

PEOPLE ARE STRANGE
Okefenokee Swamp
Corrie Mohr-Wright's Cabin
Northern Florida

The afternoon started out promising enough, beginning in Angel Falls when Ian called Corrie telling her he just received his check for the book advance and he wanted to take her someplace to celebrate. She mentioned she had a cabin in the swamps of Okefenokee National Wildlife Refuge known as "The Land of Trembling Earth." Perfect – she had plans of trembling the earth anyhow. She told him to meet her at The Cove and she would drive him there.

Corrie picked Ian up in her 1967 cherry red Camaro convertible. She put the top down once he got inside. The drive from The Cove proved uneventful, just a nice ride down long windy back roads. Corrie turned up the music knowing it would deter any conversation until they reached the cabin.

The cabin wasn't run down and it wasn't scary in the least, other than being in the middle of the woods next to nowhere. This cottage was cozy, very comfortable and clean with a state of the art kitchenette and big screen TV on the wall of the living room. No bags, no muss, no fuss. Corrie and Ian quickly found the bedroom.

Ian sat on the edge of the bed.

Corrie got up and pulled the curtains closed and slipped out of her dress, then turned off the lights. The place was enshrouded in darkness.

"Hey, it's almost too dark to see," Ian said.

"I thought you did your best work in the dark," she replied.

By the end of the evening, Ian was sleeping naked in the queen size bed. Too much wine, too much sex and he was out like an amateur boxer, lying on his back, but happy.

Corrie pulled on a black slip and tiptoed so as not to wake her lover, she picked up his pair of khakis, opened his wallet and looked at the check for the advance issued by Norton & MacKenzie. It was bigger than her last two advances.

She wanted to scream. Instead, she picked up Ian's wrist and sank her sharp fangs into his flesh. Unlike the previous rendezvous, she bit down savagely, blood spurting all over the place.

Ian, startled from sleep by pain saw Corrie pull his wrist to her mouth and start sucking, drinking his blood: biting him like a starving shark, drinking his blood like a thirsty alcoholic. He thought he was in the middle of some bizarre nightmare – this didn't make any sense whatsoever. She was a writer, not a vampire.

She leaped from the wooden floor onto the bed, straddling his chest. She bent down and started biting his neck. She hit the carotid, blood spurted on the backboard and pillowcases.

Ian screamed, but it was useless. The nearest neighbor was much too far away. His screaming grew weaker and weaker, and then finally stopped. If his heartbeat could be amplified, it would sound much like his screams, weaker and weaker like the last beams of a flashlight before it died.

Corrie bit into her own wrist, blood squirting. She held the bloody wrist above his dry lips. "Drink up or die," she ordered as the red droplets dripped into his mouth. She brought the wrist closer to his lips. He latched onto it, drinking it like a hungry infant who hasn't been fed for days, slurping, sucking, and gurgling the blood down.

"Welcome to my web, said the spider to the fly," Corrie sang in the low lit room. She turned on the lamp beside her on the nightstand.

Ian realized he was lying in bed, fully dressed, and there were no bloodstains anywhere. No bite marks on his wrist or neck. He had a hangover. He thought he had drunk too much the night before, but remembered only having two glasses of wine.

Corrie was also fully dressed in a tight red dress sporting spaghetti straps.

"Did you put some hallucinogens in the wine?" he asked rubbing the sleep out of his eyes.

"Nope, not at all, lover boy," she crooned. "That sounds like something your character Preston Whitehouse might do in *Ask Twice* – not my style at all. I'm more direct and to the point."

"It was far too real for a dream," he retorted.

"And that leaves just about one possibility."

"That it was real? *Bullshit*! You're not a vampire!"

"I'm not? Why so?"

"Because I saw you in the daylight."

"Did you?"

Ian thought about it, then thought about it again. The lectures and all their meetings had been during the evening. The time he went back to her hotel room was also during the night and that time he didn't wake up until the following night.

"Okay. I guess I haven't seen you in the daylight. Big deal. You're a night owl."

"You still don't believe I'm a vampire."

"No." This time he said it with less conviction.

Corrie turned to face Ian directly. Her green eyes changed to a shiny gray. Fangs jettisoned out of her mouth, sharp as daggers. She picked up his wrist and sank her teeth into them. She drank the warm blood, leaving a red stain across her face.

"Jesus Christ stop – that frigging hurts," he cried out. He tried to get out of bed, but a pain bolted up his leg and he couldn't move.

"No use in trying to leave," Corrie slurred. She pulled back the covers and he saw his left foot was chained to the metal bedpost.

Ian was almost too stunned to reply. He cleared his throat and finally said, "I'm sorry, but I'm not into bondage."

She chuckled. "Don't flatter yourself. You are chained for other reasons. Try to pull the chains off."

He grabbed the chains and his hands felt like they were on fire. Smoke emitted from them. "What the hell –"

"The cuffs are made of iron and the chains are made of silver, which can kill a vampire and –"

"And I'm a vampire –"

"You catch on fast. Yes. Blood drinkers, blood lovers for eternity. Your blood is mine. My blood is yours."

"So you chained me up to kill me?"

"Perhaps."

"Just great. I make it as a writer and end up getting killed by a vampire."

"If I wanted to kill you, I would have done that last night when you were still human. Look at your hands ."

Ian looked at the same hand, not a single burn mark was on it.

"What the —"

"We have accelerated healing."

"Regeneration?"

"Don't be absurd, we're not lizard people. We're still human…ish."

"Huh?"

"Our bone marrow has been modified — but if you lose a limb, it's gone."

"So that is why decapitation kills a vampire?"

"You catch on quickly."

"Why did you turn me into a vampire? I don't understand this. It doesn't make any sense. Why give me eternal life?"

"More like eternal damnation and loneliness." Corrie chuckled again. "You get the pearl in the publishing business and I get the empty shell in return. Now you are going to have eternal life to deal with my anger. It seemed like a fair trade."

"I can give you my advance if that's what you're after —"

"I don't need your money. I have plenty of my own."

"How did you first become a vampire?"

Corrie snarled. "None of your goddamn business."

"What else can kill a vampire?"

"Decapitation, as we already talked about, and a stake in the heart. But those things would kill a human too. And of course sunlight. I didn't do all this just to teach you the ways of our kind. That is the end of today's lesson, class dismissed."

She didn't want to talk anymore about the undead and Ian was letting everything sink in. The silence seemed to tick for an eternity between them.

Corrie returned with a chalice of scarlet syrup.

"What do you want from me? You don't want my money. You don't want to have sex with me –"

Corrie whirled around. "Did I say that? You are chained and now are my sex slave. It's the only thing you're good at. That and being a food source: blood and sex, a delicious combination, and after I'm done with you, I will leave the window and blinds open and the Sun will turn you extra crispy and your ashes will blow away in the Southern winds. But first, let's start with the sex."

"Not tonight, I have a headache."

"The only headache you are going to have is here," Corrie said caressing his crotch.

It was storming. The rain battered on the cabin's tin roof.

She unzipped the back of her dress and it slid to the floor. She was wearing a matching set of a leopard print bra and panties. "Meow," she purred doing her best cat impression.

"That is hot," Ian agreed, undoing his pants and unzipping his zipper. "Why don't you crawl towards me like the cat-woman you are? I want to hear you purr throughout the night."

Corrie crawled on the foot of the bed, her hands on the mattress, inching slowly forward towards Ian, stopping in front of his erect crotch.

"You like what you see?" Ian asked.

"Yes!" she said with a salacious smile.

"Why don't you finish undressing me, if you want to see more –"

"My pleasure," she whispered as she started tugging off his black briefs.

Ian grabbed the chain and quickly wrapped it around Corrie's neck. Her flesh began searing.

"Stop that!" she screamed. "Goddamn it!"

"Give me the key," he demanded.

Reluctantly, she pulled it out of her bra.

Ian's hands sizzled like a steak on a metal platter. He unlocked the chain around his foot with one hand. Then locked the cuff around her ankle and released the chain.

She rubbed where the silver chains had been wrapped around her neck, the marks quickly healing.

He walked over to her purse and opened it, then he and took out some car keys. "These must be the keys to your Camaro?" Ian asked.

"You better not leave me here and steal my car. You bastard! If you thought I was angry before, now I am full-throttle pissed off!" she shouted. "I should have killed you. I will make sure you regret this for the rest of your eternal life."

The cabin door slammed shut.

"You have no idea what I'm capable of –"

The only reply was the sound of her car starting up and peeling out.

CHAPTER NINE:

MANEATER
Okefenokee Swamp
Northern Florida

The muscle car was built for speed and Ian was hurtling down gravel roads in the swampland, determined to get the hell out of Dodge.

He had to think. He had to form some kind of a plan. He didn't know where to go or why. He was driving dangerously fast, with no destination. All he wanted to do was put himself as far from that bloodsucking bitch as possible.

An alligator flashed in the headlights' glare, crawling leisurely in the middle of the gravel road. Ian swerved, but the muscle car spun and skidded off the road, landing in the middle of a bog. The car was stuck in sludge. He tried his cell, but couldn't get a signal. He couldn't call a tow truck or Elaine or anybody.

"Shit!" Ian screamed as loud as he could. "Shit and *shit*!"

He rolled down his window. The night was full of sounds of the swamps – the sad songs of the cicada, the buzzing of mosquitoes, the who-ing of owls, and the creepy deep bellows of alligator mating calls.

"Freaking sounds like *Animal Planet* out here."

He hit the accelerator and mud flew everywhere. The wheels weren't getting any traction; tires were spinning round and round fast, but going nowhere equally fast. Ian sat there in the darkness and wondered "What would Preston Whitehouse do in this situation? How would he get out of the mud?"

Ian pondered the situation as a dragonfly flew by the passenger window and a mosquito bit his hand.

"I'll let some air out of those tires of yours old chap, let's say, about 20 psi each, so I can still drive safely, but have some added traction in the mud. And then, I'll drive the car in reverse, adding more traction and maybe get out of this sludge-hole, ole chap. It really isn't that bloody difficult. You're going to need a tire gauge of course, to make sure you let out the proper amount of air."

Automatically he went for the one he kept in his car, but this wasn't his car – this was Corrie's. He turned on the overhead dome light and noticed bright neon pink seat covers. "Jesus!" Ian swore, "Those flipping seat covers are so bright, they're burning my retinas!"

He opened and searched the glove box compartment: maps to Florida and Georgia, the driver's manual, matches from some place called Kitty's Lounge, and at the very back a tire gauge.

He gingerly stepped out of the car, but, try as he might, he sank up to his ankles in murky mud. "Aaarrghhhhhhhhhhhhhhhhh! This is not my mother flipping night!"

The croaking of bullfrogs sounded as if they didn't really care.

"You gotta calm down ole chap." It was his Preston voice talking to him. "You got to remain cool and collected if we are going to get out of this alive. Okay?"

He yanked his foot out of the sludge and sprang onto drier ground.

After catching his breath and calming his nerves, he waddled into the mush and systematically let the air out of each tire – getting muddier with every wheel.

After finishing the last tire, he noticed a pair of ruby red eyes shining in the swamp water. These eyes glowed because of the reflection from the car's headlights that were left on. An alligator emerged from the murky water and started to chase Ian.

He remembered doing research for the Preston Whitehouse thriller about what to do in such a situation, learning he should try to run zigzag. So he zigzagged as fast as his two legs could take him, as the alligator snapped at him.

Ian made it to higher ground, looking down at his car. The gator gave up the chase and crawled back into the murky waters.

He made it back to the Camaro and shifted it into reverse. He slowly pressed the gas, finding a little traction, but that was all it needed to move backwards. He kept backing up slowly, until his back tires hit the gravel road again. He shifted into drive and drove to the top of the bluff overlooking the swamp.

There he took out his cell phone. The call was answered on the first ring.

"Ian?" Elaine asked crying. "Where the hell have you been?"

"It's a long story –"

The sobbing grew louder. "You haven't called me for three days. I texted you over a hundred messages. Every time I called your cell, I kept getting your voicemail over and over and over again –"

"Honey, I can explain –"

She kept crying, but managed to keep talking. "I filed a missing persons report with the police because I was so goddamn worried. Your car was parked at a two-hour spot downtown and they towed it and I had to get it out of impound. I couldn't eat or sleep—"

"I'm in a lot of danger right now. And you might be too –"

"What?" She was crying and trying to talk at the same time, making anything she said incoherent.

"Listen. Pack a couple of suitcases. Stuff whatever clothes and our belongings in them as quickly as possible and stick them in the back of the car. Can you do that?"

"Yes. Okay." The sobbing started to slow down.

"Lock all the doors and windows."

"Okay. Be careful. I'm scared and worried at the same time. Love you –"

"Love you too. I'll be home shortly."

Ian stuck his cell back into his pocket. He needed some tunes to brighten up his spirits. He turned on the dome light and the radio, but out in the swamplands he couldn't get any clear channels, just static. He noticed there was a CD player which he knew had to have been installed later, because '60s Camaros didn't have compact disc players. He looked around for some CDs. Behind the sunvisor he saw a plastic casing but only one disc labeled "80s Mix." Loading it into the player, the song "Dead Man Party" by Oingo Boingo started playing.

In a few hours he'd be home.

He drove slowly down the bluff, gravel popping and pinging the car with little metallic clicks as dust clouds swirled in the rearview mirror.

Finally he made it onto the highway.

The open road, a muscle car, and a night full of stars. It might not be such a bad evening after all. He was driving down the dark highway for about fifteen minutes when he heard an explosion from beneath the car that started the automobile sliding to the right. He slammed on the brakes and got out to investigate. Luckily this time there were no alligators around. Unluckily, he had a flat tire.

He tried the phone again, no signal. "Can anything else go wrong with this frigging night!" he groaned into the darkness.

CHAPTER TEN:

WHO CAN IT BE NOW?
The Strange Residence
Angel Falls, Florida

Elaine sat nervously in the kitchen at the smooth rectangular white oak dining table, staring at her pink cell phone, waiting for Beethoven's famous 5th Symphony notes to play from Ian's ringtone. Instead she got more silence.

A loud thunderclap exploded overhead, startling her. Then lightning crackled against the sky. Rain began pouring down hard.

She heard a very unusual sound – like hail beating against the windowpanes of the French doors. That was followed by a constant scratching sound.

"Oh," Elaine said to herself. "That must be Harley, the neighbor's Doberman." The dog would occasionally mosey over from next door for some attention or snacks or simply company.

When she walked to the doors, she noticed they were locked. She pulled back the blue curtain, but there was no dog. Corrie was scratching her fingernails up and down the glass, her auburn hair blowing in the storm. Her eyes gazed, like a cobra before the strike.

Elaine double-checked to make sure the door was locked. It was. The gun was in the bedroom. Before she could turn to run, the doors flung open and Corrie leapt in.

"So this is where Ian deposits his sperm when he isn't screwing me," Corrie said.

"What?"

"Your screams are going to be delightful accompanying this storm."

Corrie didn't want small talk; she wanted blood. She jumped on top of

Ian's wife and savagely bit her neck again and again with her razor sharp fangs. Elaine's life fluid composed an abstract artwork of her death on the walls and carpet.

CHAPTER ELEVEN:

HEART LIKE A WHEEL
Northern Florida
On A Highway
A few miles from Okefenokee Swamp

Ian opened the trunk, hoping the spare tire wasn't going to be one of those donut tires. He was lucky; it wasn't. Having a flat tire was bad enough, but par for the course of the night, the spare tire was flat too. He took the flat spare and walked down the road thinking there must be a gas station nearby. Wrong again; the nearest service station was ten miles away, Gus' Gas, which looked like it was built in the '70s when petroleum prices first soared sky-high and hadn't been successful since. And, of course, it was already closed. However, an automatic air compressor machine waited on the side of the building. He fished around for some change and filled the tire to 20 psi (to match the other tires on the car) and rolled it down the road again, another ten miles, before getting back to the car. He took out the tire iron and loosened the lug nuts. Then he put the tire jack under the bumper and jacked the Camaro high enough in the air. He took off the lug nuts (putting them in his pocket, so as not to lose them), took off the flat tire, and replaced it with the newly pumped up spare. He twisted the lug nuts back on, tightened them, pumped the tire jack to the ground, and put the bad tire in the trunk.

As if he didn't have enough grime on him, changing the tire was a dirty and messy job and he was tired. He took a couple of deep breaths, collecting his thoughts and wits again and got back into the car, he pulled out his smartphone, and the screen lit up.

"Hello lover boy," the woman answered. It wasn't Elaine; it was Corrie. Then he realized he must have dialed his former mistress' phone number by mistake. He hung up and redialed the number.

"Hello lover boy … again. You didn't dial the wrong number. This is your wife's phone," Corrie said.

Ian checked the nameplate and it displayed Elaine Strange's name and the number.

"Where's my wife?" he shouted.

"Lying on the carpet with her neck savagely ripped apart."

Ian was too choked up to even respond. Tears were running down his face. He tried to wipe them away, but more would follow.

"Remember when we screwed at your place when your wife was out of town? I didn't forget where you lived. I wanted to have so much fun destroying you. You stole my car, stole my career. Now I'm going to steal your life."

The tears quickly stopped as he grew angry. "I killed your career and you killed my wife. I think that is a fair trade."

"No, no, no" she said. "So far, you've gotten off lightly."

"I'm not afraid of you," Ian said lying. He cleared his throat so he could sound tougher. "What are you going to do? Jump through my cell phone as we speak. By the time you get to where I am right now, I could be in Mexico or Canada before you even got here."

"Wherever you run, I will follow you. I will follow you in the darkness. I will follow you to the end of the world. Wherever you hide, I will find you. There is no escape …. None," she spat before hanging up.

There was no other sound, except for the beating of Ian's heart. He heard it banging like a speed metal drum solo. His mouth was as dry as funeral dirt. He was hyperventilating. He was profusely sweating. He would probably die on the spot, if he wasn't already dead.

"Think," he said to himself. "What would Preston Whitehouse do?"

"That's an easy one chap," His voice changed. It sounded like a fifty-year-old British man who had smoked too many cigarettes, drank too many gin and tonics, and had too many one-night stands. "I'd high-tail it out of here. She's at your house in Angel Falls; you are here at the Okefenokee Swamp in Northern Florida. You are three hours away. You have a three-hour lead-time on her. It will take her another three hours just to get back here. By the time she does, you will be three hours some other direction."

40

"That's true," he pondered. "So where do I go so she won't find me?"

"Do I have to answer all of your questions, chap?" his Preston Whitehouse character chuckled. "You have any friends who live far away – really far away?"

"Yeah a few. I have an ex-girlfriend who lives in Tennessee."

"That is brilliant ol' chap. What's her name?"

"Heather Platt," he said.

"What a ghastly name."

"She was the looker in high school. Still is from the photos posted on her Facebook. Heather went out to Hollywood shortly after we broke up to become an actress. She wasn't able to break into show business. To make ends meet, she became a goth stripper, calling herself 'Countess Trouble: Mistress of the Night.'"

"Where is she living at in Tennessee?"

"Chattanooga, Tennessee. Performs at a strip club called Grin & Bear It."

"Chattanooga is about five hours from here chap," considered Preston, "and eight hours from Angel Falls. Sunlight destroys vampires and it will be dawn before that time. So we better get a move on. We will have at least a day's head start. Oh, one last thing."

"What's that?"

"This vampire is a crafty one," Preston warned. "Cunning as a cobra and deadly as a hungry shark. She was able to get to Elaine from the time it took you to get stuck and unstuck in the mud, get a flat tire, get another tire fixed and change your tire."

"I'll be careful," Ian promised himself. Then Preston disappeared to the far corners of his mind. He was left alone in the stolen Camaro and with a mission.

He started up the car and soon was speeding down the road. The first destination was back to Gus' Gas so he could air up all the tires and after that, the open road North to Tennessee.

CHAPTER TWELVE:

I TOUCH MYSELF:
Grin & Bear It Strip Club
Chattanooga, Tennessee

The Grin & Bear It Strip Club entrance looked like a twenty-foot bear head. Customers entered through the mouth to get inside. It was a dark, dank room permeated with the smell of spilled beer, cheap perfume, and sweat. The ten tables and two booths were dwarfed by a long stage with a brass pole in the middle. Christmas tree lights were strung all over the sides of the small stage. On the wall next to the stage was a goofy grinning neon grizzly bear sign with the words: HOT DAMN! HOT WOMEN! flashing on and off beneath. Definitely not a classy gentlemen's club; this was a sleazy strip club all the way.

Ian sat at the table closest to the stage with the bottle of beer he had bought after entering the establishment. There weren't many patrons left in the club, only a drunk middle-aged man with a short gray beard at the bar and an old man with several empty beer bottles at his table staring blankly at the stage.

The announcer said, "And for our last dancer, we have Countess Trouble, Mistress of the Night. She comes all the way from Transylvania and wants to suck your blood and other things. Give it up for Countess Trouble!"

The goth-rock song "Bela Lugosi's Dead," by Bauhaus started playing and fog began rolling across the stage. A movie screen descended from the ceiling and the 1931 original Dracula movie started playing, but it was manipulated with negative lightning effects to give it a creepy and dark look. For the next two minutes a strobe started flashing, the movie was played, but no one appeared. It was a good thing nobody in the audience was epileptic or they would have gone into a seizure.

Countess Trouble strutted onto the stage. She was short, barely over five-foot tall without the heels she wore. She had long dark brown hair with red tints. She was wearing a long black cape draped over her body, but the audience couldn't see much else she wore except the red nine-inch stiletto shoes. Bauhaus' loud haunting music hung heavily in the air and Trouble danced rhythmically to the beat of the song. She pranced around the stage, then standing in front of Ian, she opened her cape; she was sporting a matching black leather bra and g-string panties set. The bra had skulls on each of the cups, and the panties had one of those biological hazard toxic waste symbols between her legs. She was also wearing long black gloves and spider web stockings.

Ian spotted a butterfly and flower tattoo that covered most of her left arm. On the back of her neck was a tattoo of a bat. He wasn't sure if it was supposed to be a vampire bat or the creepy bat featured on the label of rum. On her left inner thigh was a tattoo written in Old Script style that said, "Until the day breaks and the shadows flee." He guessed that was suppose to be scary, but he knew it was a passage from the Bible.

At this point Trouble unfastened her bra and let it fall to the floor. The screen went back up. Bela Lugosi was still dead and the song was over. The song "This Corrosion" by The Sisters of Mercy started playing. She pranced over to the pole, and climbed up about half way, then spread her legs wide in the air as she twirled round and round like a carousel of flesh.

Ian clapped. He was the only one in the place who did.

She climbed off the pole and danced slowly to the edge of the stage, above Ian's table.

"Remember me?" he asked.

"Yeah," she answered nonchalantly, chewing her gum with the beat of the song. "How could I forget?"

He fished through his pocket and threw a twenty-dollar bill on the stage. Trouble picked it up and put it on the side of her g-string.

"Can we talk?"

"I can't socialize or fraternize with the customers. I can get fired for that."

"Oh I'm sorry. I didn't know."

"Throw down some more cash," she whispered.

"Okay." He grabbed another twenty and tossed it on the stage.

This time Trouble bent over directly in front of him, her behind high in the air. She turned around and softly whispered, "My shift is almost finished. Meet me at the IHOP down the road in a few minutes."

The music finished and Trouble exited the stage. A heavy-set bald man with a big beard, wearing jean shorts and a loud Hawaiian shirt, took the stage. "Let's hear it again for Trouble – I'd like to get *in* that kinda Trouble," he snickered at his own joke. "My name is Lee The Eel, I'm the announcer and owner of Grin & Bear It. This is last call for alcohol. Thanks for your patronage and hope you come again soon. And I'm talking about returning to the club. You don't have to go home, but you can't stay here," he chuckled.

Ian threw a five-dollar bill on the table and left.

The International House of Pancakes was less than "down the road." He could've easily walked this distance, but he figured it was safer not to leave the car in the lot and maybe get Heather in trouble. He thought about it for a moment and laughed at his own pun: Trouble. Maybe that's how she got her name.

Ian sat in a far booth. He wasn't sure if the pancakes were that internationally known or not as he drank a mug of coffee. As Trouble walked in, he almost didn't recognize her until she scooted into the seat across from him. She was wearing a pair of jeans and a white blouse; her long dark and reddish hair was pulled back in a ponytail and she had on black plastic-rimmed glasses that were shaped like cat eyes.

"It has been a long time, Heather –" he started.

"I no longer go by that name. I'm Countess Trouble, Mistress of the Night. Or you can simply just call me Trouble."

"Okay Trouble. I'm in a lot of trouble –"

"So for help, you come to Trouble to help you with trouble? That doesn't even make much sense."

"I'm being chased –"

"By a band of Ninja Clowns?"

"What?" Ian asked confused.

"A band of Ninja Clowns. That was the excuse you once used when you wanted to go parking down by the lake," she said. A waitress stopped by, but Trouble waved her away.

"Yeah, I vaguely remember that," he smiled. "No, by a vampire."

"Ninja Clowns are more believable than that *Twilight* crap."

"I'm in grave danger —"

"Grave danger. Vampire," she chuckled. "I get it. So you have Robert Pattinson chasing you? I could even kick his skinny, pasty ass —"

"It's not Robert Pattinson —"

"Oh, it's Taylor Lautner. Wait, he played the werewolf. Now, that guy has a body. He could chase me anytime he'd like —"

"No — it is a female vampire."

"A Tinkerbell with fangs?" She chuckled again.

"I'm totally serious."

"You drove a long way, just to get laid. Why don't you just go back to your wife?"

"She's dead."

"Dead?"

"The vampire murdered her. Now she wants to kill me. I just need a place to crash for a couple of days, until this blows over."

Trouble thought about it. "I don't know."

"I helped you out when things were falling apart in Hollywood. And you never paid me back a dime. Just for a couple days? Okay? Don't make me beg. I'm not a good beggar."

"You bought me an airplane ticket so I could go to Des Moines for my mom's funeral. And you were even engaged at the time." She thought for a moment. "I suppose I owe you. Remember it is just for a couple of days. Yeah, you're always nice to me in and out of the bedroom. One of the few guys in my life to do that."

"I can't thank you enough Heath —"

She gave him a disapproving look.

"Uh, I mean, Trouble," Ian corrected himself.

"I live with my grandmother, but it's cool. I live in the basement and she's old and deaf and can't hear anyway. I have a bar, pool table, bedroom, and even a hot tub. It isn't much, but you are welcome to it."

"You don't know how much you're helping me. Perhaps even saving my life. I can't thank you enough," Ian repeated as he paid for the coffee.

46

They walked to his Camaro and drove away.

CHAPTER THIRTEEN:

STAY THE NIGHT
Trouble's grandma's basement
Chattanooga, Tennessee

Taking off clothes for a living, Trouble disrobed very quickly. Her blouse landed on top of her Persian cat, Truffles, who fled the room; her black bra hung from the doorknob, her jeans were on the bookcase, and her black g-string slipped to the floor. The only thing she still had on was her glasses. She crawled into her four-poster bed. Her head was on a fluffy pillow, her derrière high in the air. "Do me like an animal," she panted.

"No," Ian gently nudged her and she went down onto the mattress on her back. "I'm going to do you the old fashioned way."

"Same thing."

He took off his shirt and climbed on top of her. His pants and shoes were still on, but it didn't matter. He opened his mouth and a pair of sharp fangs sank into the tender flesh along Trouble's throat. He drank her blood as she had orgasm after orgasm.

When Trouble regained consciousness, he was dressed again and she was wrapped in her blankets. "I think I came so hard, I blacked out."

He laid his head in her lap, looking longingly into her eyes. "All we need now is a picket fence and a dog and I'll have everything. Everything my heart desires."

She laughed softly. "Living in my grandmother's basement is hardly the American Dream."

"The American Dream died when we first went to the Moon. It was replaced by the Material Dream."

Ian walked over to her bookcase. Most of the books were trashy romance novels. He took out two paperback books and brought them back. *Midnight Blue* by Nancy Collins and *The Lunatic Café* by Laurell K. Hamilton. "These are the only bloodsucker books you have," he said. "I suppose we can read these for research. Which one do you want?"

"*Midnight Blue*," she said grabbing the book. "I'll read it as I take a bubble bath."

About an hour later, Trouble returned wearing a white terrycloth robe. Ian was on the bed reading his book.

"Did you learn anything?" he asked.

"Not really. Vampires can wear sunglasses after dark."

"Interesting. I wonder why they do that."

"To be cool. It wouldn't hurt to be a little more cool now, since you are a bloodsucker."

"I'm not cool?"

"You dress like someone who works at Home Depot."

"I have some dark sunglasses."

"I'll keep that in mind."

"So how did you become a vampire?" she asked.

Ian smiled. "To sum up: We met, we talked, we met again, we drank, we screwed, we talked some more, I got published, she got dropped and pissed, turned me into a bloodsucker too, I locked her up, she became free somehow, she killed my wife, now she is after me. And here I am."

Trouble stared and squinted her eyes. "Could we maybe fill in the commas?"

Ian chuckled and began again – the whole story, especially the commas.

"That was an incredible story, just like *Titanic* with fangs," she said.

"It is nothing like that movie. But it is like the ocean liner: we've just hit an iceberg and the Captain has said, 'Good, now we have ice.'"

Trouble giggled.

"We should be headed for bed."

"Yes," she yawned.

"One last thing."

"Yeah?"

"I'm going to take you to a real nice place to eat tomorrow evening. Where is there a fancy establishment to dine at?"

"The Chattanooga Choo Choo."

"The song?"

"Or course it was a song, but at one time it was also a train. Or more specifically a train station. Now it is an overpriced restaurant and hotel for tourists or for couples with a lot of money. But let's go to the Tennessee Aquarium, too. They are both close to each other."

"Lovely, sounds like a plan."

CHAPTER FOURTEEN:

TRAIN IN VAIN
The Chattanooga Choo Choo
Chattanooga, Tennessee

Ian was dressed in his khakis, a white shirt, and metallic blue tie, looking like an employee from Staples. He had to borrow Trouble's younger brother's clothes that were stored in boxes in the basement, because his clothes were stained with mud. Trouble was wearing a strapless black dress that blended in with the dusk sky. They only had about an hour to explore through the Tennessee Aquarium before it closed, and since the River Journey Building was the largest freshwater aquarium in the world, with over a million gallons of water in its tanks, this was no easy task. They rushed through as fast as they could, but only managed to see breathtaking jellyfish, blue catfish, octopi, sea otters, Japanese spider crabs, alligator gar, barramundi, giant whiptail rays, and sharks. Ian couldn't take his eyes away from the black eyed beasts swimming in the tanks

Ian and Trouble barely made their reservations in time. Chattanooga Choo Choo was once a majestic and opulent train station from the early 1900s that had been converted into a high priced hotel and restaurant complete with a neon train sign on its roof.

The entry to the station house restaurant was once the railway baggage room. Ian and Trouble were seated at a table near the stage. Their waitress was Diana, a young lady in her early twenties who could easily pass for a younger version of Gena Lee Nolin from *Bay Watch* if the TV actress traded in her swimsuit for a black cocktail dress. As one of the Singing Servers, she had to divide her time between the tables and the stage, which wasn't that difficult for their table. Trouble ordered a shrimp scampi dinner with Sauvignon Blanc wine. Ian on the other hand, was on a strict liquid

DARK CITIES: DARK TALES

diet and only drank Pinot Noir.

After she finished savoring her meal, they sat admiring the grandeur of their environment. He kept thinking of Leo Tolstoy's *Anna Karenina*, in which a disastrous train accident foretells the doomed heroine's plot and demise, and she kept thinking of the movie *Polar Express*.

He softly held his hand in hers.

"Remember when we took English class together, in high school, in Des Moines?"

"Oh yes," she smiled. "Mr. Van Dyke."

"I called him Dick Van Dyke, because he was such a dick. But there was one love I took away from that class, besides winning your affection in the backseat of my dad's Ford, a love for F. Scott Fitzgerald."

"I thought you hated *The Great Gatsby*."

"I did at the time. It was just a melodramatic love triangle. What I loved was the fluidity of Fitzgerald's words, how they freely flowed like bourbon from a bottle into a shot glass. I wish I could write with such a paradigmatic flair. I'm just a meat and potatoes writer. But after that class, you went west to pursue your dream as an actress and I headed south to go to college to become a writer."

"Yes," she said with just a touch of melancholy and regret in her voice. "Both off and on the road to success. Mine came to a dead end."

"Mine wasn't much better, really. I went to Angel Falls University to study English, until my father found out and said, "No son of mine is going to end up with such a penniless profession as a writer." So I became a Political Science major with a minor in English. I took a work-study job as a Student Supervisor at the C-Store, the college's convenience store and spent most of my time working on a book. After graduating, I became Assistant Manager and between all of that, I wrote and finished my book."

"I always thought you were a good writer, even back in high school. Remember that poem you wrote for me?"

"Yes I do." He thought for a moment, then recited "Your eyes are like the purple dusk of twilight and my heart is filled with embers that burn with passion throughout the night. Or something like that."

"Wonderful," Trouble said. "I have to go to the ladies room. After you pay the bill, let's hit one more place before we head home."

"Where's that?"

"Coolidge Park Carousel."

"A merry-go-round?"

"Yes, it will be fun. It's better than the one we went on our first date at Adventureland, remember that?"

"Yeah. I recall that. We had fun, riding on those horses going round and round like a spinning clock."

When Trouble left for the restroom, Preston Whitehouse decided to make his appearance.

"Hello, old chap," Preston commented. "Remember that bloodsucking bitch that killed your wife. What's her name again?"

"Corrie Mohr-Wright."

"Yes that's her."

"What about her?"

"Remember when she said, 'wherever you run, I will follow you. I will follow you in the darkness. I will follow you to the end of the world. Wherever you hide, I will find you. There is no escape … None,'"

"Yeah."

"Wherever can be Chattanooga, Tennessee. Playing date night with a stripper isn't running."

"I told her, I will just take her on this merry-go-round and we'll go after that. What's the harm?"

"Your funeral chap," and Preston suddenly disappeared.

"Excuse me, sir," Diana, the waitress said. "I didn't realize you were on your phone."

Ian cleared his throat. "It's okay. I just finished the call."

At that moment, Trouble returned to the table.

The waitress handed him the bill.

He glanced at it, dug out his wallet, and gave her his credit card.

A few minutes later, Diana returned to the table. "Sir, I am sorry but your credit card has been declined."

"Really?" he looked surprised. "I know this trip has been expensive. Here try this credit card instead," he said getting another plastic card from his wallet and handing it to her.

A few minutes later, the waitress returned back. "I'm sorry sir, but that credit card was also declined."

"I'll be damned!" Ian said angrily, but softly.

"It's alright," Trouble said, fishing for a credit card in her handbag. She found one and handed it to the waitress. "We're sorry about that. I should have given you this card in the first place."

A few minutes later, Diana returned with a receipt. Trouble added a tip and signed it.

They left in silence as a cold autumn breeze blew in the dark night.

"Is there an ATM around here?" he asked.

"Yeah across the street."

"I'm going to withdraw the money and pay you back."

"Don't worry about it. My treat."

"No, I insist."

He took out one of his ATM cards and punched in the secret numbers and the withdrawal amount. Instead of dispensing cash, it only dispensed a receipt.

"Shit!" He said more angrily this time. He did the same thing with two other ATM cards. Ending up with the same results – no money, just receipts.

Ian looked at Trouble. "She must have cleared out all my bank and joint accounts and credit cards, thousands of dollars now gone. That bitch took everything. Everything."

"Who?"

"The vampire who is after me, the one who killed my wife. She must have found all the information from my records at the house."

"I'm sorry."

"Wait a minute," he snapped his fingers. "She didn't take everything." He opened up his wallet and took out a check and showed it to Trouble.

"Jesus!" she swore looking at the check. "That's a lot of money."

"That's the advance for my book. I will endorse the check. You take the money I owe you for the bill and some for your time and trouble, and we'll call it even. How does that sound?"

"Okay, but like I said, it's my treat, I make good money taking off my clothes. Let's not talk about money anymore. We'll cash that check later."

"I'm still worried about that psycho vampire bitch after me."

"She took the money and ran. Probably is in some resort at Key West living high on the hog on your cash."

"Probably," he mumbled.

"The night is still young," Trouble added with a gentle smile. "Let's catch a ride on the Coolidge Park Carousel. My treat, I can afford it, it only costs a buck."

They walked over the Walnut Street Bridge, a pedestrian crossing over the Tennessee River that led to the other side and went to the Coolidge Park Carousel, a wooden blue and white pavilion with a golden horse weather vane on the roof. The merry-go-round featured handcrafted animals, such as horses, turtles with shields, cats, giraffes, bears, and rabbits. Calliope music played overhead as the animals spun round and round. Ian and Trouble sat in a golden booth bound together arm in arm.

The ride was like a blast from the past; it was like they were teenagers again at the Des Moines amusement park. After it ended they walked back over the bridge, planning to go to Market Street, where they had parked the Camaro, and go back home.

Halfway over the bridge, Ian heard a familiar voice. "I'm not going to get tossed aside like a used condom!"

He turned around and saw Corrie standing next to him, holding the silver chains in her black leather gloved hands. She hit him in the shoulder with the chains, where it burned his skin. Smoke seeped from the wound and it sounded like bacon frying for breakfast.

Other pedestrians on the bridge started to scream and run.

"How did you get out of those chains back at the cabin?"

"I had a spare key in the other cup of my bra." Corrie brought the chain down again. This time it hit him in the right leg, bringing him to the ground, where she hit him repeatedly. She whipped him almost a half dozen more times; each time the silver chains burned him more and more.

Still lying on the bridge, Ian kicked out at Corrie knocking her to the ground too. But she quickly got back on her feet to fight. She brought the chains down hard again, this time across his chest.

More people were screaming and fleeing the bridge.

At that moment Trouble did a roundhouse kick and Corrie went back down again.

Like a cat, she was quickly back on her feet. Corrie slapped Trouble so hard she went to the ground instantly.

Ian knew this was his chance. He knew that fighting Corrie was useless. She had the silver chains and he had nothing to fight back with. Instead of defending himself, he fled. He climbed the metal fence and jumped over it to the rapid, murky Tennessee River below.

Police sirens could be heard blaring in the distance. Corrie suddenly ran over the bridge. Trouble was in a state of shock; couldn't believe what she'd just seen; she kept looking at the river below trying to catch sight of Ian.

CHAPTER FIFTEEN:

MY NAME IS MUD
Trouble's grandma's house
Chattanooga, Tennessee

Trouble was crying on her sofa in the basement when she heard someone knocking on the side door. Her grandma had gone to bed hours ago and she knew no one would be visiting at the wee hours shortly before dawn.

She switched on the outdoors light. Standing outside was Ian, covered head to toe in dripping mud. He looked like someone who might have taken a dip in the chocolate factory, but instead, was covered in soot and grime and smelled like a fish aquarium that should have been changed three weeks ago.

"Ian," Trouble cried and ran to him, hugging him tightly. "I thought you were dead."

"Reports of my death are greatly exaggerated," Ian deadpanned. "Okay, I'm ripping off Twain, but I couldn't help it. Of course, I'm not dead. I'm undead. There are only three things that kill a vampire – stake through the heart, decapitation, and sunlight. Luckily for me, drowning isn't one of them."

"I was so worried about you," she kept crying. "I saw you swept down the river and –"

"I'm just a little messy, but I am alright. Second time in twenty-four hours I ended up covered in mud. But at least this time I didn't have to run from an alligator."

"What?" she asked, confused.

"Long story. I will tell you some other time. It's okay," he said, stroking her hair, getting it all muddy in the process. "I'm making a terrible mess."

"Let's take a shower together."

"Okay."

They shed their clothes on the landing and walked downstairs naked, taking a long, hot steamy shower together. After using up most of her shampoo and bottle of body wash, they were both clean again.

After the shower, Ian wrapped himself in a Cradle of Filth beach towel and Trouble slipped into a black terrycloth robe. After drying himself off, he realized he was in a dilemma.

"Trouble."

"Yes, dear."

"All the clothes I own were on my back, but now are on your floor, and they're ruined. I have nothing to wear, the rest of your brother's clothes don't seem to fit me."

"We'll just cash your check and you can buy all the clothes you want," she explained.

"When I jumped in the river, the check was ruined."

"Dammit!" she snapped, and then paused. For the longest time she didn't say a word. "I have an idea. My ex-boyfriend has some clothes in the closet and he's about the same proportions as you – well, above the waist that is." She winked.

Several minutes later, Ian emerged from the bedroom. He was dressed in black leather pants, a greasy black leather biker jacket, and rattlesnake boots.

"I guess I should have warned you, he's a Goth freak," she said with a giggle. "In the upper right hand pocket of the jacket, there are some black sunglasses; put 'em on."

Ian fished around the jacket, found the shades and slipped them on.

"My God, you look exactly like Andrew Eldritch, circa 1989."

"Who?"

"The lead singer for The Sisters of Mercy."

"Never heard of them. Are they a gothic girl band?"

Trouble decided not to correct him.

"I couldn't find a shirt."

"He didn't wear one. He loved showing off his pecs."

"I don't have great pecs to show off."

Trouble gave him an appraising glance. "Your pecs are okay."

"I can't go out in public shirtless."

"I can give you one of my shirts."

"Okay, I will go out in public without a shirt. Now what am I going to do next?"

"Get a shirt?"

"No, I mean about my life. I have no money. No car. No wife. Nothing."

"You have me."

"Yes, I have you," he said, holding her. The embrace lasted several minutes.

"I suppose I could call Guido."

"Guido?"

"Guido 'The Gecko.'"

"What kind of name is 'The Gecko?'"

"It's an alias."

"Of course it's an alias. What kind of man has an alias?"

"Someone who doesn't want people to know his last name in case someone squeals to the police."

"Jesus –"

"No, it's Guido."

CHAPTER SIXTEEN:

DEAL WITH THE DEVIL
Grin & Bear It Strip Club
Chattanooga, Tennessee

Guido "The Gecko" looked like a cross between Elvis and Tommy Lee Jones. The pompdour hair added to the image of The King and so did the sneer, but the rest was definitely Tommy Lee Jones. The only thing that didn't look like either the world famous '50s rockabilly singer or the famous Academy Award winning actor, was the nose – which looked like it belonged to an old boxer, because it had been broken many times. He was dressed in an expensive gray suit that was too nice for a sleazy strip joint. He sat in the far corner, drinking a glass of red wine when Trouble, wearing a black summer dress, and Ian entered the Grin & Bear It club. Some stripper named Candy was dancing to the song "I Want Candy."

Guido nodded his head when he saw the couple. "Let's go into the office."

Lee The Eel was wearing his trademark loud shirt, sporting reading glasses, sitting at his desk counting the night's proceeds when all three walked into the room.

"We need your office," Guido said.

"Okay," Lee said quickly. "Take as long as you like."

"You betcha your ass I will."

Lee hurried out of his seat, leaving the piles of money on his desk and bolted from the room.

"You look like some kinda Goth freak," Guido said staring at Ian. "The type that shits bats. But you are exactly the kind of boyfriend I'd imagine my lovely Trouble would go out with. Either of you want a drink?"

Both shook their heads no.

"When I was about your age, I was on this flight from Chicago to San Diego. Anyway, the guy seated next me was an auditor from the Internal Revenue Service. Imagine, me next to an IRS guy – the IRS are the ones who put Al Capone in the joint. Anyway his job was to go around the country auditing businesses. He had plenty of interesting stories. But one story in particular was very fascinating. You see, this guy had to audit a brothel just outside of Las Vegas. He checked their books and the usual stuff and then he went through all the dirty and soiled towels. Figuring each customer used a towel or two, and to see that it matched with the brothel's records. Anyway, the story broke loose in the IRS and any undesirable job got the nickname 'Towel Duty.' I have a Towel Duty job for you."

"We are with you so far," Trouble said. "Please go on."

"I'll get to the point. Trouble said you need some quick cash. I have a job. You drive this Lexus to a chop shop in Chicago. The owner there is this guy name Lorenzo The Lizard. He will pay you once the car is delivered. I'd do it myself, but I have three strikes."

"So ol' chap," Ian said, using his Preston voice. "How many bills is a job like this worth? If I'm driving all the way to Chicago, I hope it's bloody well worth it."

"I'm not sure how much Lorenzo will pay you. But it will be worth your time, you can trust me on that. Trouble, you never told me he was British."

"I –" she started to say.

"That a problem, old chap? Because I used to live across the pond?" Ian stepped a little closer to Guido.

Guido shook his head no. "Not a problem at all. Our steering wheels are just on the opposite side of the car. I have another story for ya two. Okay?"

"Sure chap. Your last story was very entertaining indeed."

"When I was a teenager, I fell hard for this pretty young girl named Holly who lived in my apartment building in the Bronx. Anyway, I always hung out with Holly and we kissed all the time. One day, she said she would give me a hand job. Both of our folks were home, so we couldn't do it at our places, so we decided to do it under the stairs in the basement. She unzipped my fly and was yanking away, until this old lady came down the basement to do her laundry. Anyway, Holly freaked out and quickly zipped up my zipper real quick. The only problem – my junk was still hanging out. It got caught in the zipper, which was painful as you can imagine. We had to call 911 and some old man had to get my cock freed from the metal clasp of the zipper, which was also embarrassing. Long story short – don't yank me on this job. Don't embarrass me on this job. Don't screw this up, because I will hunt you down like a dog and force you to dig your own graves. Capeesh?"

"Capeesh," Ian and Trouble both said at the same time.

"Here," he threw the keys to Ian. "It's the gray Lexus in back." He handed a piece of paper to Trouble. "This is the address of Uriah Heap in Chicago."

"Thanks again, Guido," Trouble said, giving him a kiss on the cheek.

They exited out the back and, unlike the front of the club that was a giant bear's head, the back was just two doors; luckily it wasn't a giant bear's butt. The Lexus was easy to spot in the parking lot. There weren't that many cars left and it was the newest one.

"I didn't know you could talk like a British person," Trouble teased as she walked to the passenger's side of the car.

Ian hit the unlocked button on the remote. "Don't you remember? I took acting in high school," he lied.

"No." She slipped into the leather seat.

He started the engine and they drove off into the night.

CHAPTER SEVENTEEN:

THIS OLD HOUSE
Trouble's grandma's house
Chattanooga, Tennessee

The trouble with old houses is they are always settling and make all kinds of strange noises in the middle of the night. Abigail was used to unusual noises at all hours, but this particular noise was really strange, something completely weird for her old house: it sounded like someone was scratching at her windowpane. At first she thought it might be her granddaughter's cat Truffles. The feline sometimes clawed at her screen when it was climbing to get to the roof. But Trouble had taken all the screens down two weeks ago and replaced them with storm windows for the fall and upcoming winter. Abigail felt a cold blast of air; trying to figure it all out, she turned on the lamp on her nightstand.

"Heather?" She said, calling to her granddaughter. Then she put on her bifocals she kept on the headboard. The first thing she noticed was that the bedroom window was open. The second was a woman standing next to her bed. She blinked, thinking her old eyes were playing tricks, but a woman with long auburn hair that glistened in the moonlight and catlike eyes was staring at her.

"Who are you?" Abigail asked, trying to sound brave, but her voice was filled with fear nonetheless.

"Your worst nightmare," Corrie hissed before biting into the old woman's jugular with her sharp fangs.

CHAPTER EIGHTEEN:

DRIVE

Trouble's grandma's house
Chattanooga, Tennessee

The plan was simple: Trouble was going to write her grandma a note saying she was going to be gone for a couple of days as she went to Chicago. She'd pack a few things, then Ian and she would hit the open road to the Windy City.

The first thing they noticed when they pulled the Lexus into the driveway was that the side door was open. Not a little open, but wide open. Trouble knew she had locked the door when they left. The couple quickly got out of the car and ran into the house and to her grandma's bedroom. That door was also open and they could see blood all over the bed, bed sheets, and mattress. Abigail's neck was savagely ripped apart. Written above her bed, in blood:

NO ESCAPE

"Why would anyone kill my Nana? She was the sweetest woman on earth. I don't understand it."

Trouble started crying and Ian held her tightly. He didn't really have an answer, he just stroked her hair as the tears continued.

"What does 'No Escape' mean?" she choked out between the tears.

"It is something that Corrie said to me. It's a warning. We can't stay. She might be watching us – it could be a trap."

"But I can't leave my Nana like this –"

"I'm sorry. We've got to go. We'll call the police after the job is done."

For the next several hours Ian and Trouble didn't talk. She was silently sobbing; he was lost in the darkness. The night had swallowed them both as they drove on I-65 North.

"Again, I am sorry for the loss of your grandmother."

"Thanks," That hit her ninja dagger star thrown through his heart. Between sniffles and tears. "She was the only family I had left. Besides Uncle Dan in Davenport. I'm also sorry about your wife."

Trying to think of something positive to say, he replied, "Life is the most positive thing you've got and, unfortunately, I took mine for granted. Didn't learn that lesson until it was too late."

Her only response was to caress his cheek.

"The magic of youth dissipates as we grow up. But I firmly believe in our golden years, we hold on to the last spark. Only a few sparks of those tiny embers are all we can hold on to, but they still hold all the magic. I never met your grandma, but I imagine those embers burned bright in her."

"Yes, she was just like that," she said softly, barely able to speak.

"Sometimes it's hard to see the sunshine when there are so many dark clouds. But it will get better, babe, it will get better."

For the longest time, they drove in silence. Finally Ian spoke again. "We'll make the bloodsucking bitch pay for this. She killed my wife. She killed your grandmother. And we are going to kill her."

They drove in silence until they reached Indianapolis.

"Remember we used to talk about going to that club in Chicago all the time when we were teenagers? What was the name of it? Do you remember?" Ian asked.

"The Metro."

"Yeah that's it. After we do this job, maybe we should stop by for a drink. What do you think?"

"Yeah," she said softly. "That would be fun."

"Elvis has left the building," Ian said, doing his best Elvis impression. He paused. "To get a ham sandwich."

Trouble giggled.

The streetlights were becoming fewer and far between in this section of town. It was dark and gloomy in a city that shone so brightly.

Ian pulled the Lexus into an abandoned gas station. The building was all boarded up. The gas pumps had been removed. An empty truck trailer sat parked on the side and it was the only thing in sight.

"Why are you stopping here?" Trouble asked.

"We are about three hours from Chicago. I've been driving all night. I'm exhausted. We really can't afford a hotel or motel. I thought I'd sleep in the back of the trailer. I can't sleep in the car because of sunlight. Besides, I'm starving and could really use a late night snack."

"I'm hungry too. But I don't see anywhere we can eat."

"I wasn't talking about we, but me," he said, pushing the lever to her seat. It reclined so far back, the headrest nearly hit the backseat. He unfastened his seatbelt and hers too, then unbuttoned the front of her dress. She was wearing a black bra. He lifted up the cups and proceeded to squeeze and lick, and lick and squeeze. Trouble kept her eyes closed and moaned softly with pleasure.

She quivered only slightly, when he sank his fangs into her breast and started drinking the blood flowing freely from the wound.

"I love you–" It slipped out of Trouble's mouth, like a slippery condom on a Prom Date.

"I love you too," Ian replied. "When you left for Hollywood to pursue your dream of becoming an actress, my heart didn't break. It stayed with you the whole time."

He starting drinking her blood again. After a few minutes she suddenly said, with a shortness of breath, "I don't feel that good."

A memory hit him like a grand slam during the World Series. "You're anemic, aren't you?"

"Yes," she acknowledged.

Ian realized he was putting her life in danger by drinking her blood. As hungry as he was, he didn't want to do that.

He helped redress her.

"We'll get something to eat first thing tomorrow night. I'll sleep in the trailer."

The truck trailer was really old. The doors in back barely held on. When he started walking along the inside, he could see several holes in the side and the roof. At dawn, this would leave him extra crispy.

He walked back to the car.

Trouble was lying on the backseat, curled up to sleep.

"The trailer has too many holes in it. I'm going to sleep in the trunk," he said, pushing the button to unlatch the door. He gave her the keys. "See you tomorrow night."

"Okay," she said sleepily.

The trunk was filled with bags of cocaine, marijuana and laundered money. He moved some of the bags around, and crawled inside. He used the bags of cash as a pillow, before shutting the door again.

CHAPTER NINETEEN:

URIAH HEAP
Abandoned gas station
Indianapolis, Indiana

It was a cold, damp, rainy fall night as the wind whipped its chill across the prairie and plucked a million bits of color from the trees, sending them all spinning into the gray stormy night. Lightning crackled across the dark sky, illuminating the multi-colored leaves lost in the desolate atmosphere.

Trouble was awakened by a tapping on the window. At first she thought it might just be the wind blowing against the glass, but realized it was a knocking and then thought it was Ian.

When she opened her eyes, she discovered it was neither, but rather a tall, black man pointing a Ruger-SP101 .38 Special gun at her. She screamed.

"Shut the hell up," the man said. "I'm not going to hurt you. I just want the car."

She stopped screaming.

"That's better," he said. "Don't do anything stupid or I will gun you down through this window. Okay?"

"Okay," she quietly agreed.

"Good. Now. Unlock the door."

"You promise not to hurt me?"

"Yes."

She opened the back seat door the stranger slid in and shut the door quickly. "Where is your boyfriend?"

"My boyfriend?" she repeated surprised.

"Don't play stupid with me, missy. I know who you are. Where you are going. Everything. Your boyfriend, Ian Strange?"

"We got in a fight," she said, saying the first thing that popped in her head. "And he left me."

"Out in the middle of nowhere, in the middle of the night?"

"Yes," she said, with more conviction this time.

"I thought the British were a little more polite than that," he said, mulling on the whole situation. "Look. Let's just say: that Guido has taken a lot of work from me in the past. I was supposed to do this job, but he gave it to you instead. I plan to still do it. Give me the keys."

She thought for a split second about turning on the car and making a mad dash for it. But she knew the bullet would find her before she even turned the key.

She handed him the keys. He grabbed her arm, shoving the gun next to her chest. He opened the backdoor, shoving her out, then opened the front door and pushed her in. He jumped in the driver's seat and started the car.

"You know all about me. Can you at least tell me your name?"

"Othello."

"From Shakespeare?"

He didn't answer.

Othello drove off from the boarded up gas station and back onto the highway.

In the dark trunk, Preston Whitehouse made an appearance. "Things are all buggered up," he said softly.

"Yes," Ian answered quickly. His voice was also quiet, but full of panic. "Some rival gangster name Othello has taken the car at gunpoint. Trouble is in trouble. What are we going to do?"

"Remain the hell calm, is my advice, old chap," Preston replied. "Look, he might have a gun. Big deal. Guns don't kill vampires. And he doesn't even know you are in the trunk. When they open the trunk, jump like a leech onto a leg and drain him dry."

"Would that work?"

"Why wouldn't it, old chap. You're about three hours from Chicago. He'll get his in due time."

"Okay."

"Don't worry about this bloody Othello," Preston added. "I will take care of everything."

The whole trip to Chicago, Trouble avoided eye contract with Othello. She looked out the window, getting lost in the speeding scenery in the dark nightscape until they pulled onto Interstate 94 and she saw the "Welcome to Chicago" sign on the highway.

Othello drove down the interstate until they entered Chicago, the Windy City. He pulled off in the Southside, on a dark, rundown street where most of the houses were boarded up. The only place that wasn't abandoned was a small neighborhood used car lot with a sign out front that said Uriah Heap. He flashed the headlights three times, and the garage door to the repair shop rolled opened. A tall, middle-aged black man carrying a wrench walked up to the driver's side door. He was wearing coveralls with the nametag "Big Lar" on it, and was still in pretty good shape for a man who turned sixty about three weeks before. "What the hell are you doing with this car? I thought Guido gave this gig to someone else."

"He did. But I decided to do it instead. Do you have a problem?"

"No, not all. Why don't you pull the car into that stall over there," Big Lar directed, pointing to the closest one. "Unload everything on the bench over there. I have your money in the office." He walked away. Othello pulled the car into the assigned stall. "I just need to finish some business. Be back shortly." He pushed the button to open the trunk and walked around. When he pulled the trunk door open, Ian jumped out and on top of him, slamming him against the cement floor, smashing his head repeatedly. There wasn't much left but a bloody pulp afterwards. Blood and bits of brain matter splattered the floor. Ian quickly took out the drugs, money, junk bonds and weapons, stacking them on the bench. After he was finished, he opened the passenger door and Trouble hugged him tightly, although his leather jacket was covered with blood.

Ian and Trouble walked into the dimly lit office of Big Lar.

"Who the hell are you?" the black man asked.

"Preston. Guido sent me. Where's my bloody money?" he said in his British accent.

"What happened to Othello?"

"I smashed his bloody head in on your cement floor. Listen wanker, I don't have all bloody night. Just give us the money and we'll be out of here."

He got up and peeked out the door.

"I'm charging extra to clean up that mess," Big Lar said, taking one of the piles of money and putting it in his pocket. He handed Preston / Ian four big stacks of wrapped bills. "Guido said you might need some transportation back to Chattanooga. I don't have much left, inventory is getting low. That's why I wanted the Lexus. I do have an old hippie van. It isn't much, but there's some beer in the cooler in the back of the VW. Just give me back one of those stacks and it's yours. "

Preston gave him one of the stacks of money. Big Lar handed him the keys.

A green day-glow 1972 Beetle Volkswagen Microbus was parked in the lot. It had psychedelic paintings of flowers and peace symbols on the side and even a Grateful Dead "Keep On Trucking" bumper sticker.

Ian and Trouble got inside of the old van which smelled of pot, patchouli and moldy incense.

"You said you have an Uncle in Davenport?" Ian asked.

"Yeah, Uncle Dan."

"Do you think he'd let us crash with him for a few days?"

"Sure. He's a great guy. He has some rental properties. He might let us stay there."

"Davenport is only three hours away. We can stay at some roadside motel and drive into town the next night."

"Okay," she said. "But I'm starving."

They went to a Golden Nugget restaurant; Trouble had some pancakes and coffee, Ian just had coffee.

Before they hit the road, Trouble's cell phone rang. It was the theme song from *Swan Lake*, which also was used in the Bela Lugosi *Dracula* film.

"You didn't yank me," the man said on her cell phone.

It took Trouble a few moments to realize it was Guido referring to the handjob incident.

"Big Lar said you did a great job, even pulled the hammer on Othello who has been a major pain in my ass for years. I decided to give you an added bonus. Check your Paypal account."

She switched apps, almost stunned when she saw how much was deposited in her account.

"That's a lot of money Guido."

"It's nothin', Sweetcheeks," he said with a laugh. "If you and your freaky British boyfriend ever wanna do another job for me, you know the number," he said, before hanging up.

"That was Guido," she told Ian. "He gave us a bonus for the job."

"Really. How much?"

She showed her phone with the new balance.

"Sweet Jesus, that's a lot of money," Ian said.

They didn't make it to Davenport. It was too much driving for one night. About twenty minutes from the Quad Cities, they stopped at the Crescent Motel. The neon sign had a circular moon with a Vacancy sign lit, not too surprising since the place looked empty. Just a semi-truck and a Honda Civic were parked in the lot. They could afford to go to some place nicer, but time was working against them, the night was melting away as fast as a spilled Margarita on a Texas sidewalk at high noon on a summer day.

The room was cheap enough; Ian and Trouble had the last room on the bottom floor. Clean bed, no bugs. When they went inside, they heard the moans of the other two guests. The groans were suppose to sound like pleasure, but they really sounded more like: "Hurry up, you been screwing me all night and I want to go to sleep."

Trouble crawled into bed and went quickly to sleep.

Ian walked into the bathroom and splashed some cold water on his face. He sat on the tub, listening to what was going on in the next room.

The moaning and groaning finally came to an end.

And then Ian heard some guy say, "That was the worst piece of ass I ever had. Your money is on the nightstand and I am not giving you the whole amount, either, whore." The girl cried.

The door slammed. The truck started and drove off.

The girl got on her cell phone. "Yeah, this Liz. No, he didn't pay me the full amount. I don't know. I can't come up with that kind of money, I'm broke." She started to cry again and hung up the phone.

A half hour later, Liz Half Price the prostitute went to sleep.

Preston made another appearance.

"She's asleep – you are starving. Get another late night snack?"

"How?"

"In a place like this, those windows should pry right open old chap. Break into her room, drink some blood. You don't have much time. It's probably about only thirty minutes before dawn."

"You hear yourself? This sounds like a bad plotline from the book."

"You have no choice."

"Okay," Ian said reluctantly. "So what are we going to do about Corrie?" he asked.

"I've been thinking about that. I am tired of being the prey. I think we should become the predator."

"What do you mean?"

"She has been after you for some time now. You've been running from her. Instead of running from her, run to her. Confront her, a final conflict, once and for all. You need to rest up first, of course, after you finish up drinking the slapper."

"Slapper?"

"British slang. Sorry about that. Will explain later." Preston disappeared and Ian was looking at himself in the mirror.

Ian quietly opened the door.

The window to the next room pulled open easily and he crawled in.

Liz was lying on top of her bedspread and she was completely naked. He couldn't get a good gauge of her age, because it was still dark in the room, but he guessed she was in her mid-thirties with dishwater blonde hair and an incredible figure.

Ian gently picked up her wrist, bit into it, and was drinking blood quickly. He got his fill – blood was smeared all over his face.

He was about to leave when she woke up.

"Who are you?" she asked sleepily.

Ian froze. He didn't know what to do. But it was okay, because Preston kicked in.

"Milady, I am a vampire and I just drank your blood."

"What did you call me?" she said rubbing her eyes.

"My lady –"

"Are you British –"

"Yes."

"A British vampire?"

"Yes."

"I always thought vampires were hot."

"I've got to go."

"I'm still horny from my last john. I'll give you a freebie."

"Really. I've got to go."

"Please, I drove all the way out here. I got stiffed on some money. I just want a good screw so I can get a decent night's sleep for a change."

"Milady, I should really go."

"Please." She got up on all fours. "I've been a bad girl. Do you want to spank me?"

"Uh. No."

She started crying again.

Preston went down on the bed and gave her a hug. "It will be alright milady."

Liz quickly put her breasts in his hands. "Just one kiss?"

She stuck her tongue in his mouth before he could say anything. At the same time, she unzipped his black leather pants and began stroking his cock.

She pushed him between her legs, moaning softly and Preston entered her. The hunger for blood was getting out of control. The bedsprings whined in protest. He sank his teeth into her neck. The moans became louder and warm delicious blood flowed into his mouth.

She came and came again. Sunlight was only minutes away.

"I gotta go, I know you said it was a freebie, but do you have a business card or something? When I can get my British money turned into American cash. I will pay you handsomely. "

"I work an escort service," she said, handing him a business card. "The name is Eliza Stuckey, but everybody just calls me Liz. "

He took off his watch and gave it to her. "You can pawn this and get your money back in the meantime."

She looked at the watch. "It's a Rolex –"

He zipped up his pants and walked out the door as the Sun began to rise; it was burning his eyes and face, black smoke snaking in tendrils from his face. He quickly slammed the door to his room shut. His face still burned, but it was no longer on fire. With his remaining strength he crawled onto the chair sitting by the wall and fell asleep.

CHAPTER TWENTY:

TROUBLE IN RIVER CITY
Government Bridge
Davenport, Iowa

No rain. No storm. It was a nice autumn evening as the hippie van drove over the ironclad twin-deck Government Bridge that spanned the Mississippi River, between the states of Iowa and Illinois. Also known as the Arsenal Bridge, because it provided access to the Rock Island Arsenal on the Illinois side, the largest government-owned weapons arsenal in the country, it was the first railroad bridge to be built over the Mississippi. The top deck was used for the trains, the bottom for automobile traffic, and the draw span opened for barge traffic. But we are jumping a little ahead of ourselves –

The evening actually started back at the Crescent Motel. Ian woke up lying uncomfortably in his chair. Trouble was sitting on the bed watching TV.

"You're awake," she said with a smile. "Your face was badly burnt this morning, but it's all healed now."

"Trouble, I have to tell you something," he said in a quiet tone.

"Yes."

"I went next door last night, broke into that girl's room and drank her blood. The sun was starting to rise and that's why I was burned so badly."

"Duh. You're a vampire. You're going to need to drink people's blood. With my medical condition, I can understand why you would drink other people's blood. I'm okay with it, I just don't want to hear about it."

"I love you."

"I love you too," she said. "I called Uncle Dan. He wants us to meet him where he works."

"Which is?"

"The Source Book Store. It's a used bookstore, downtown Davenport. He owns it. The store should be closed, but he will stay there, waiting for us."

The hippie van pulled in front of the Source Book Store, which was nestled between several other stores and shops. Across the street was the Wells Fargo Bank, that building with the clock tower, the largest building in downtown Davenport.

The owner, Dan, was a mild-mannered middle-aged man, who wore wired-rimmed glasses and a charming smile. He looked more like someone who would teach Calculus II at a Community College, but was doing some inventory of the books when Trouble and Ian entered the store, which was jam-packed with books. It was warm and cozy, a place bookworms loved.

"Heather," he said, giving Trouble a warm hug. "And you must be Ian Strange. Didn't you use to date years ago?"

"Yes, sir," Ian said.

"I'm Dan or Uncle Dan – no sirs here, I work for a living," he chuckled.

"Okay, Dan. Yes, we used to date in high school in Des Moines."

He shook the young man's hand. "I'm glad to finally meet you. You made Heather happy back in high school. I am glad you two are an item – is that what they call it these days?"

"Sure, Uncle," Trouble giggled.

"Heather said you need a place to stay for a bit. I have some rental properties; most of them are rented right now, but I do have a two-story brick house across from Riverview Terrace –"

"Lookout Park, aka Make-out Park?" Trouble giggled again.

"The view there is splendid, the area is built on a bluff."

"A bluff?" Ian asked.

"Built on a bluff and has been operating that way since," Dan joked. "There is a three-acre park and you can see all of downtown Davenport, Iowa and across the Mississippi River to downtown Rock Island, Illinois," the bookstore owner said with a warm smile.

"Sounds lovely," Ian commented.

Dan handed the keys to the place to Trouble. "There is only one drawback."

"What's that, Unc?" she asked.

"I had the place painted a few days ago. It still smells of paint."

"That won't bother us. Thanks a million," she said.

"Yes, thanks again, Dan."

"No problem. The new tenants won't move in for another three weeks. If you stay longer than that, I can make some other arrangements."

"We're just staying a few days."

"In that case," Dan said. "Before you leave, we must have dinner, the three of us."

"We will Unc," Trouble said hugging him.

"Thanks again," Ian shook his hand.

CHAPTER TWENTY-ONE:

LATE NIGHT SNACK
Uncle Dan's Rental Property
Riverview Terrace
Davenport, Iowa

All the traveling made Trouble tired. She crawled into bed and fell asleep. Ian sat on the Fainting Couch, wondering what to do. He was still hungry, hungry for blood. *Only one thing to do,* he thought. *Go out for dinner.*

Ian drove around the Quad Citie searching for prey. He saw some streetwalkers in downtown Davenport, but wanted something a little more challenging.

Patty O'Neil was from out of town at the Midwest Ladies' Bowling Tournament, which was being held in Davenport. Her team, the Bolingbrook Bowlers (from Bolingbrook, Illinois), were celebrating by drinking and gambling on the riverboat casino. At forty-something, she was divorced, slightly overweight with a good paying job, over-ample breasts, and the best blonde hair color that she could afford.

The Bolingbrook Bowlers had petered out by ten p.m., just before midnight Patty was still gambling and drinking. At the Witching Hour, she decided to go back to her hotel before another day of rolling the ball down the lanes. She decided to walk across the Davenport Skybridge, to check that out before hitting the sack.

Ian had seen the Skybridge when he was driving the hippie van down River Drive. It was a spectacular sight, waves of colored lights brightly reflecting in the night overhead. The bridge's best feature wasn't the lights, though, but the outstanding panoramic view of the river and the night cityscape from the floor-to-ceiling, mostly glass walls, five floors up. Nicknamed The Bridge to Nowhere because the bridge didn't really lead to anything particular.

Patty enjoyed the view, staring out at the night and looking at the colorful lights inside the Skybridge. There was no one else on the bridge this late at night. She had seen enough and was ready to turn around to leave when she saw a tall man standing almost next to her, which startled her.

"I'm sorry I startled you," he said. "The name is Ian. I'm from out of town and saw this bridge and the colored lights and decided to check it out. I was captivated by you. I didn't mean to stare."

It had been awhile since anyone had hit on Patty. She smiled. "My name is Patty. Also from out of town." She pointed to her black and gray bowling shirt that had her name stitched in it below the MLB patch. "That stands for Midwest Ladies' Bowling. My team came in second place today."

"Congratulations."

"Thank you."

"You are very winsome."

"Win some? Lose some – that is the nature of bowling," she brayed. "And even won more on the slots," she laughed.

Ian thought for a few seconds and said.

"You are very fetching."

"Fetching or not, I am old enough to be your mother – almost. Mary Ann and Peggy on our team are closer to your age. I can introduce you if you like."

"They may be younger, but I doubt I will find someone so attractive. I know people don't use words like winsome or fetching anymore, I'm a writer."

"A writer. Really. I wonder if I've read any of your books?"

"My first book is coming out soon."

"I guess you should be getting the congratulations."

"Let's both celebrate."

She giggled. "I've already had enough to drink to last three nights."

"I wasn't talking about alcohol." He moved closer to her, locked his eyes on her eyes, not blinking. "And I want you."

Patty suddenly realized she wanted him too. She gulped. "My hotel is just on the other side of this bridge."

"I can't wait that long," Ian said. He kissed her. Hungrily, like a starving animal. His tongue entered her mouth, slithering inside like a serpent ready to attack.

"I don't sleep with strangers. Actually, I haven't slept with anyone for a long time. But I am drunk and I find you very attractive. But let's not do it so all of Davenport can see us, I might have to play here again next year. At least, let's go over there in the far corner."

"Okay," Ian said taking her hand and walking into the corner. It wasn't dark, because the multi-colored lights were flashing overhead.

He started unbuttoning her bowling shirt. He pulled up the cups of her bra, licking and kissing her right breast. He lifted up her skirt, pulled down her panties.

"Do you have any protection?" she asked between pants.

"Like from a stake?" Ian quizzed her. "No."

Without further hesitation and before she could stop him again, he entered her and bit her neck at the same time. Both felt incredible. The lights overhead were shades of crimson as Patty came and came and Ian kept drinking her blood until he came.

Ian re-dressed and buttoned up Patty's clothing.

Patty handed him a business card. "If you are ever in the Bolingbrook area, give me a call."

Ian took the business card and left into the night.

No longer hungry, pleasantly high on Patty's blood, Ian returned to the rental house and in a darkened room fell fast asleep.

The next night, when Ian woke up, Trouble said, "I'm starving. Let's go to Front Street Brewery."

Getting slightly lost by a block or two, the hippie van turned down a side street, right across from the Government Bridge. There was smoke in the back of the van. Trouble quickly took out a couple cans of beer from the cooler to put out the small fire.

They got out of the vehicle and walked to the corner of Rockingham Drive.

"There is a place called Front Street Brewery, near the Arsenal Bridge," Trouble said. "They have great beer and food."

"Sounds good. Let's go."

It was a cold fall evening in downtown Davenport. The sky was gray and cloudy, with leaves blowing in the sky. Ian and Trouble were sitting at the front window of the restaurant/brewery. It was a brick building nestled in the Bucktown area of town, home to the Bucktown Center For The Arts which housed several art studios and shops featuring the works of local artists. Ian was drinking a pint of Raging River Ale, a commemorative named after the Mississippi River Flood of 1993.

Nearby, at the intersection of Fourth Street and Pershing, Corrie sat stewing inside of her Camaro. She was under an old rusty reddish brown iron railroad bridge covered with graffiti. Under the bridge was a multi-colored mural with musical notes and a drawing of a trumpet horn. On the other side of the bridge was the luxurious Hotel Big Chief. The area looked like a place where someone would get gunned down for a drug deal turned bad. Corrie was waiting for her moment to strike, and she knew it should be soon.

In the restaurant Ian took another sip of the beer. "God, this is delicious."

The warm interior of Front Street made them feel welcome. The burnished wooden floors, tables and booths were a contrast to the exposed brick walls. It was the kind of place where everyone knew your name, if they weren't out of state visitors.

They looked across the street at the Mississippi River.

"This is the closest I have ever been to the river," Ian commented.

"Tell me about your Great American novel," Trouble said.

"I don't know if I'd call it that," Ian said. "For one thing it is set in the Caribbean, and for another, the protagonist is British."

"Does it have cathartic ending? And everyone lives happily ever after?"

"Nope. The protagonist goes on vacation to relax and doesn't relax for one moment on his trip. And there are no happy endings in life – we all die a sad and painful death, nothing happy about that."

There were seagulls flying next to the Government Bridge. He hadn't even known there were seagulls in the Midwest, especially during winter. They heard a screeching of metal. It was a freight train slowing down across the street, going under the Arsenal Bridge. Something about the way the train was moving so slowly gave them the creeps. All the boxcars were the same – red and rusty with no name of any companies on them.

After the French dip and French onion soup were devoured by Trouble, they walked back to the van.

Trouble climbed into the van and Ian went in the back to grab the last two beers.

Corrie observed the two as they exited the restaurant. They sure seemed damned happy about something – maybe the food or atmosphere. Good thing, too, because it was the last laugh he'd ever have. Her grip on the silver chains tightened. Through blinding anger a smile played at the corners of her mouth.

As Ian fished through the watery ice in the cooler looking for the last beers, he glimpsed a glint of shiny metal in the van's window and ducked just as silver chains whooshed by his head into the van's inner panel with a sharp clang. Grabbing the tire iron, he maneuvered himself around Corrie and dashed down a bridge walkway. He stole a glance over his shoulder. Corrie was hot on his trail, waving the chains like some crazy lasso. It amazed him that she didn't hit herself swinging them around that way. In fact, he kind of hoped they would hit her; at least that would slow her down for a few moments.

Trouble's heart leapt into her throat when she saw Corrie in the side-view mirror approaching Ian with something shiny in her gloved hands – a chain of some kind, she thought. She fumbled with the seat belt as she watched. "Stupid piece of shit!" she shrieked, yanking it. *Okay, stop*, she thought. She took a breath and squeezed. The belt popped open and she pushed the door open, practically falling out of the van. She recovered and sprinted after them, trying to close the gap. A police officer holding a gun was coming up fast behind Corrie and she knew this scenario wouldn't end well – for the officer. If she could distract Corrie just long enough maybe she could buy time for Ian and that unfortunate cop. A small pile of rocks under a gate caught her attention and she picked up a handfull and began to run again. The rocks felt kind of scrawny, but usable, she decided, for what she had in mind.

Ian passed the half way mark across the bridge, his heart thundering and his mind racing for solutions. He needed an advantage, somewhere to stop and plan, a chance to –

The heavy, multi-stranded, silver-coated chains hit him in the back, knocking him off his feet. He tumbled to the ground, his back burning and the tire iron flying out of his grip, skidding to a halt out of reach. As he rolled to face Corrie, she moved in, standing over him, her face twisted in anger.

"You're finished!" she hissed, spit spraying. "A writer no more. A vampire no more. An annoyance no more. No more!"

With no way to launch a defensive, Ian threw his arms up and drew in his legs. The chains struck him again and again. He skittered backward like a crab, but the chains fell and fell again, his bones snapping and his skin burning. He tried to roll away, stretching, reaching for the tire iron, but the chains kept falling.

"Put those chains down, ma'am!" The officer ordered, his gun drawn and ready.

Corrie's head snapped around to look at the officer, chains hanging in mid-swing. Her eyes narrowed and she leapt off of Ian, charging the officer. The officer back-pedaled, emptying his gun as he went.

The echoing gun fire stopped Trouble in her tracks about a yard from the action. She threw the rocks one at a time with all her might, but Corrie didn't seem to notice, even when one hit her squarely in the back of the head. They might as well have been jelly beans. Out of rocks, she sped to reach Ian. The tire iron lay in her path and she scooped it up as she ran. This distraction was all Ian had.

Corrie examined the officer's face just inches from her own. A discolored stain began to spread from the officer's crotch. She locked a single hand around his throat and raised him off the ground, his feet dancing. She looked up and shot Trouble a glance filled with hate that said, "You're next," and, without looking at him further, she sank her fangs into the officer's neck while he screamed. When she'd finished draining him, she shook him once and snapped his neck like he was farm chicken. Then she dropped him, and he crumpled into a pile like a sucked dry juice box.

Troubled gasped, but concentrated on getting Ian to his feet. She shoved the tire iron in Ian's hand, "Go! Go! I'll keep her busy," and pushed him away. She turned to face Corrie, but Corrie was already there.

Ian stumbled and half ran, pain wracking his body, heading for a v-shaped metal pylon with a plaque on one side, large enough for him to hide behind. He glanced in Trouble's direction. Corrie lifted Trouble and flung her aside like a child tossed away an unwanted toy during a temper tantrum. Oddly, Corrie didn't snap her neck first — that was, at least, something. Trouble didn't move, but he didn't think she was dead either; at least he hoped she wasn't.

Corrie gazed in his direction with cold, gray eyes and marched toward him, swinging the chains.

Come on, come on heal, damn it! Ian thought as he prepared to wield the tire iron, stretching and flexing his damaged arm. He needed his swing to be perfect to disable her. He peeked around the wide pylon, but didn't see her.

The chain whizzed by his head and missed by an inch, sending bits of concrete flying. He scrambled to the side of the pylon and turned. Corrie was practically on top of him. He thrust the tire iron with all his might, but missed the mark, so he pulled it back. She screeched and backed away, blood gushing. After a few tries, Ian jabbed the iron through a loop in the chain, twisted, and tugged. The chain flew over the railing and disappeared into the Mississippi. He thrust the tire iron a second time. Corrie screamed, but the iron missed its mark again. She back-pedaled with the tire iron still jutting from her rib cage.

"Damn it!" he hissed, as he watched her climb nimbly up the nearby metal pylon as if it was an every day ladder.

The world and all of its wondrous sounds and imagery spun away and, for a moment, one sickening moment, he stared up her flowing skirt, at her silky black G-string and his desire stirred, threatening to fully awaken. The taste of warm blood filled his mouth and it drizzled from the corners of his lips. His heart began thundering, his pulse racing, and his groin aching —

He tore his gaze away and made himself look back at Trouble's body — lying in a heap near the dead officer. Corrie did all that, he reminded himself. Wherever she went, destruction followed. This proved enough to suppress the stream of his unsavory vampire desires and restart reality. Ian wiped the blood from his mouth with the sleeve of his shirt, tore it off, and climbed after Corrie.

Corrie reached the top platform and disappeared with a flip of her black skirt. As he reached the top, Ian peered over the edge. He could see her sprinting along the track, so he leapt up and gave chase. About half way to Corrie, he noticed that she'd come to an abrupt stop near another pylon and picked something up, maybe a pipe or rebar piece. He noticed an old, rusted railroad nail nearby and took that, though he wondered if he was bringing a short knife to a sword-fight. When he looked up next, she was charging his way.

Like knights in a jousting match, Corrie and Ian charged toward each other. At the last possible second, they jumped and metal hit metal, sparks flying. They both landed with a thud and turned toward each other. Corrie charged Ian again. He ducked and spun, taking a stab at her, cutting her skirt. She jumped out of the way and back in, swinging the length of pipe, connecting with his mid-section. The air went out of him and he folded. She hit him again across his back and he crumpled like a crushed Coke can. As she heaved the pipe for another blow, Ian rolled, stabbed the railroad nail into her thigh, and pulled it out with a spray of bright blood. She jerked away.

Ian recovered and got to his feet. He raced toward her, stabbing her in the throat. Blood sprayed his face and clothes. She stumbled backward, making a muddled, sucking sound. Dropping the pipe, she clawed at her throat and the nail fell away with a sharp clank. She turned and ran, leaving blood spatter in her wake. Ian picked up the pipe. She scrambled up the nearby pylon. He followed.

By the time she'd reached the top, she was almost healed. She stared down at him and he back up at her. He didn't have a chance to register her plan before she leapt, grabbed a corner of the pylon, and sailed in his direction. The blow hit him in the chest and he lost his grip and the pipe. As he slid, he grappled for a hold, and ended up half way down, hanging by one hand, trying to find a foothold. She slithered down until she was right above him.

"See, my darling, you can't win." She flattened her body against the pylon and brought one booted heel down on his hand.

He cried out and swung his other hand up clawing for a hold.

She stomped again.

He lost his grip and slid several more feet. He swung himself toward the platform.

She stomped again.

He swung again and let go, crashing to the edge of the platform, where he teetered for a second before falling again. He grasped for anything to break his fall, saving himself finally on the lower lip of the platform. His hands were masses of ruined and torn flesh at various stages of healing. Below, he could see Trouble getting up. At least she was okay.

Corrie climbed down and picked up a piece of rebar, which she began thrusting at him like a crazed hunter. He swung from one hand to the next, moving around to the lower pylon. She stabbed at him again and the rebar drove into his shoulder and out the other side. He cried out, but didn't lose his hold. She bent he supposed with the intent of retrieving the bar or forcing him off. He grabbed her shirt instead. It ripped where the tear he'd made earlier had been. She pulled herself backward to keep from falling and he used that and the rebar to pull himself back up on the platform. He stood on wobbly legs and yanked the rebar out of his shoulder. *We could play this game until the end of time,* he thought.

Corrie had made her way back to the pylon and was climbing again. He clinched the bloody, rusty rebar in his hand until his healing knuckles turned white. This time there were no lustful thoughts or desires, other than to kill. He raised the rebar over his shoulder, and as she climbed he chucked it at her with everything he had in him. It speared her mid-body and she screamed, but kept climbing. He had to get to her before she had a chance to pull it out. He glanced around for another weapon and picked up the railroad nail he'd had earlier.

Near the top, she yanked out the rebar and chucked it at Ian. He ducked and it missed by a hair's width, and he watched it fall and hit the water – another Mississippi fatality. When he was just a few feet below her, she started kicking him and stomping his hands, but she was still healing and sluggish. He grabbed for a place on the pylon near her mid-section and pulled himself up so he was almost facing her. He stabbed at her chest, but she caught his hand and pushed him away.

He lost his footing and slipped, hanging tenuously. *At least I haven't lost the railroad nail,* he thought with no small amount of sarcasm, which he was sure belonged to Preston. Once again, he could only watch as she climbed down and stomped his hand. He slid a few more inches, but gained a solid foothold, which freed his hands. He grabbed Corrie's ankle and yanked. She yipped, startled, and teetered. With his other hand he grabbed her skirt and pulled her down to his level. He smiled despite his situation, and let the Preston part of him say, "Milady," and watched the questioning look on her face before he drove the railroad nail deep into her chest and let go. She howled and clawed at the nail as she fell. She'd be unconscious before she hit the ground, he knew — the stake doing its work. As she plummeted time seemed to slow and their eyes met and locked one last time. He couldn't really tell if what he saw in those cold eyes was hate, love, disbelief, surprise, or some odd mixture, but he knew it no longer mattered.

She slammed into the walkway with a sound like a dog crunching on a bone.

Ian slumped. For a few minutes he stood that way gazing down on Corrie's body and her blood draining into a spreading pool. Trouble waved her hands urging him to come down. He worked his way down to the walkway.

"I saw a police car stop a couple of minutes ago. I'm sure the cops are on their way," she said, throwing her arms around Ian. "I'm so glad you're alright!"

He hugged her, "Me, too." He looked into her eyes. "I thought she'd killed you."

She nodded, "She tried, but it's just a bump on the head and a few bruises. I'll be fine."

He hugged her harder and he knew then that he loved her. "I don't think I'd have made it through this without you."

She smiled with tears brimming in her eyes, "Me, neither."

He kissed her with raw emotion and desire that made his blood run hot and his skin tingle. The kiss lingered until distant sirens lured Ian back to reality. "To be continued," he said.

Ian knelt to check Corrie's body for any signs of vampire life, or any life at all for that matter. She was unconscious but not dead, at least not vampire dead. He would love to leave her for the sunrise, but then there were the cops – always the cops. Unfortunate, he thought. With a deliberate slowness he pushed the railroad nail all the way into her heart, both savoring and cringing with every inch. After a minute of letting the reality of her death and his freedom sink in, he unceremoniously pushed her shriveled corpse into the Mississippi, and thought, *thus ends the illustrious career of one Corrie Mohr-Wright.*

His Preston side added thoughtfully, "Goodnight and farewell for you did not go gently into that good night," sometimes Ian wondered about his Preston side.

He and Trouble watched, arms around each other, as Corrie's body bobbed in the currents until it flowed into Lock and Dam 15, as if this event had been a satisfying ending to an old, grainy, black and white film where the villain died and the heroes rode into the sunset.

"Let's go," Ian said.

Together they made their way back to the hippie van, as the sirens grew louder and the spinning red and blue lights came into view.

ONE YEAR LATER:

Ian: After resting up a few days and having dinner with Trouble's Uncle Dan, he and Trouble moved into a small apartment in Davenport, Iowa. He contacted his agent, Curtis Ballinger and told him the advance royalty check was damaged. Curtis had Norton & MacKenzie stopped payment on the previous check and issued another. With the money he made from driving the Lexus full of drugs and laundered money to the chop shop in Chicago and bonus, he didn't need to find a day job for a while. He began a new Preston Whitehouse novel called *Ask Twice…Again*. After the police investigation, after the CSI had cleaned up the murder site of his wife, and the funeral had taken place, he put his house in Florida on the market. When he came to the Quad Cities again, he proposed to Trouble.

Trouble: After the police investigations were over, she was able to collect her belongings from her grandmother's house and moved in with Ian. She gave up stripping and started teaching dance at an Arthur Murray's Dance Studio in Davenport. She eventually sold her grandmother's house and split the sale proceeds with her Uncle Dan. Ian and Trouble took the money from both house sales and moved into a small one bedroom house, a few blocks away from Vander Veer Park in Davenport.

Preston Whitehouse: Was happy to return to his further adventures in Ask Twice… Again.

Guido The Gecko: Retired from his life of crime, to spend more time with his family and grandchildren.

Big Lar: Two months after the Lexus entered the Uriah Heap Used car lot (and the death of Othello), he was busted on drug charges, served time in Cook County Jail.

Eliza Stuckey "Liz": She received an appointment with some British guy named Preston Whitehouse. When she went to the café in the Big Chief Hotel to meet him, she saw Ian instead, who paid well for her services and blood. She in turned gave him his watch back after getting it out of pawn.

Patty O'Neil: Kept bowling with her Bolingbrook Bowlers and they received a large anonymous donation. The league secretary believed the donor might have been British.

Corrie Mohr-Wright: Although her body went through Lock and Dam 15, when the Sun rose shortly thereafter, *vanished* and was never recovered.

Mark McLaughlin and I are both fans of 1980s' horror movies. We wrote this tale to pay a tribute to those creepy but cheesy flicks as The Stuff, The Blob remake, C.H.U.D., Humanoids From The Deep, Critters, Alligator, Slugs, The Ghoulies and countless others.

THE SLUDGE
by Michael McCarty & Mark McLaughlin

"Aliens!" shouted New York City Police Captain Morris Price as he added more papers to a thick folder on his desk. "Goddamn outer space aliens, living in our sewers and eating our taxpayers!"

His secretary Carla rolled her eyes. "Are you on that again? Every time somebody skips town, you launch into that whole crazy alien spiel. Enough already!"

"'Enough'?" He shook the folder at her. "If you were one of these poor slobs, you wouldn't be saying, 'Enough already!' You'd be saying, 'Avenge my death already!'"

"But aliens?" Carla said. "I mean, you keep saying something's living in the sewers, eating people. So, let's say that's the case. Why aliens? Why not cannibals or alligators or mutants – or something else from Earth?"

"The sewers are filled with methane," Price said. "I'm thinking the aliens come from a planet where methane is abundant. They need to breathe the stuff – that's why they stay in the sewers. Our sun is probably too strong for them, so they keep to the shadows. And they require food, like all living things, so occasionally they catch some two-legged sushi of the homeless variety." He tapped the folder. "They'll also go after anyone else who's stupid enough to be out alone in New York late at night. Whenever there have been witnesses, they all say the perpetrators had big eyes, gray skin, and beast-like teeth and claws. Sounds pretty alien to me!"

"Let's assume for a minute that you actually know what you're talking about," Carla said. "We've got to look at the facts. These aliens of yours – they live deep in the sewers, hiding from the sun, eating our street trash and assorted other folks –oh, and breathing methane, too." She thought for a moment. Then she smiled with glee. "Hey! Methane is also called swamp gas, and I recall from some old horror movies that swamp gas is explosive. Soooo – blow 'em up!"

Price stared at Carla in amazement. "Explosives? In downtown New York sewers? The Police Department won't take chances on ideas like that!"

Carla shrugged. "Sorry! Just trying to be helpful. To hell with your aliens! I'm going to lunch."

"You do that!"

As he watched Carla walk off, Price said softly, "Yes – to hell with them."

The Police Captain knew what he needed to do. He'd have to take matters into his own hands.

He already had a fairly good idea of where the aliens' underground lair was located. The evidence room had plenty of explosives in stock from various raids on criminal hideouts. Later that night, he dropped a few hand grenades down into the sewers. The initial blasts led to a chain reaction of explosions, igniting pockets of methane throughout the sewer system.

Since those explosions blew up the domain of the aliens, that should have been the end of the story.

But, it was just the beginning.

Destroying the alien invaders would soon play havoc with the duties of Max Witherspoon, head maintenance man at Serenity Condominiums.

Max had been working at the condos back when they were just four-story rowhouse apartment buildings. This residential housing was built before World War II and eventually purchased by Manhattan Banking and Trust Urban Development, Inc. After the hundred-plus apartments were turned into overpriced condos, Max was constantly servicing the units. Fixtures and fittings always needed adjustment or replacement throughout the aging condos.

But that wasn't the worse of it. Oh no. Max's job was about to get *much* worse.

When Price's grenades exploded, a huge mess was created in the sewer systems under the condos. The aliens were reduced to sludge – a thick, steamy stew that would not die. The cellular structure of the aliens was unspeakably hearty. Mere dismemberment was certainly not enough to kill them. Eyes, noses, claws, ears, teeth and other chunks of living gore moved through the pipes, causing back-ups, clogs, flooding –

And death.

- - -

Winona Singh in unit 10D worked double shifts as a waitress at the greasiest of greasy-spoon diners because her live-in boyfriend, would-be rock star Corey White, didn't want to get a job. He would say, "The band's on the brink of stardom, babe. We'll be rolling in dead presidents any day now."

So what did he do while his hard-working girlfriend put in 12-hour days? He played his keyboard for about twenty minutes, worked on song lyrics for ten minutes, and then spent the rest of the day watching TV, playing video games, drinking beer, smoking weed, and scrounging through the fridge for something to eat.

"Did you find a job today?" Winona asked as she opened the front door. Her feet hurt and her ass ached from truck-driver pinches. Entering the living room, she saw her boyfriend passed out on the couch with a beer can in his hand and the *Gilligan's Island* theme blaring on the TV.

She was tempted to wake his drunken butt up, but instead she took the beer can out of his hand and turned off the TV. Exhausted and sweaty, she decided to take a nice hot shower.

Winona unbuttoned her work blouse and hung it from a hook on the bathroom door. She unzipped her skirt and let it fall to the floor. She was too tired to pick it up. She turned on the boombox on the counter by the sink and played some Lady Gaga. Her undergarments soon joined the skirt on the floor.

The hot water felt good against her skin. She closed her eyes, enjoying the sensation.

If she had kept her eyes open, she might have seen the black eye staring up from the shower drain. If the music hadn't been so loud, she might have heard the vicious, hollow voice within the drain saying, "Sludge lives –"

- - -

The economy hadn't been very kind to Jacob and Ava Moretti in 2B. He'd been the owner of a warehouse that went out of business. He retired after his client contracts all dried up. She was a former church organist who had to quit her job because of her painful arthritis.

Jacob sat on his recliner, reading the newspaper and grumbling to himself. He wore baggy boxers, sport socks with holes over the big toes, and a faded t-shirt with an Italian flag on it. His wife was watching a DVD of *Cheers* episodes, but he didn't care much for a bar in Boston where everyone knew your name. His wife left to go to the bathroom, and after some time, it seemed like she was taking longer than usual.

"Hey, babe!" she shouted from the bathroom. "I think the toilet is clogged. The water doesn't want to go all the way down. It's weird."

Jacob rolled his eyes as he walked to the bathroom. "So now we have a weird toilet. Great. Did you go number two?"

"No, number one. That shouldn't do anything. I think we should call Max and see if he can fix it."

"That idiot couldn't find his butt with both hands on his hips." Max waved his hand dismissively. "I'll fix it myself."

"My hero. I'll leave you to it." Ava left the room.

He picked up the plunger and started plunging with all his might. It seemed to be a major blockage of the drain, since the water just didn't want to cooperate.

As he plunged, he heard a low, strange voice say, "Sludge lives –"

"Was that you, honey?" Jacob shouted to his wife. "What are you trying to do, scare me? It's not Halloween yet."

Ava came to the bathroom door. "I didn't say anything. You must have heard the TV."

"Yeah, probably." He waved his hand dismissively again. Ava shrugged and went back to the living room.

He was ready to give up and call Max when the pipes in the bathroom began to shake. He started to plunge harder and all the water finally flushed down.

"There! I told you I could do it myself," he shouted to his wife.

"Great," she shouted back. "I'll call the *Times*. Maybe they'll send a reporter."

At that moment, the pipes started shaking again. This time, the toilet bowl began to fill up with bits of flesh and dark, stinking blood.

"Holy crap!" Jacob shouted. The blood rose to the rim of the toilet. There was no way he was going to plunge *that*.

He stepped out of the bathroom, gagging from the smell of rancid blood.

"Are you okay?" his wife asked. "What's wrong?"

"The toilet is filled with rotten blood. I think some sewer worker must have been killed and his blood got in the system somehow. I'm calling the police."

- - -

Douglas Costello couldn't believe his luck. Just graduated from college, he'd managed to land a job as a paralegal at the law firm of Channing, Reynolds & Stone. He had to trade his colorful wardrobe of golf shirts and plaid slacks for drab three-piece suits, but he didn't mind. The money was great. Of course, he needed to shave his goatee, which he planned to do that morning, his first day of work. He'd plugged in his electric razor and was starting to shave when he heard the bathroom pipes shake, like the building was caught in an earthquake. But, this was New York, not California. He quickly turned off the razor.

Just then a long gray finger tipped with a sharp claw shot up through the sink's drain and sank into Douglas' neck. It pierced his jugular vein and within seconds, he was bleeding like a pig in a slaughterhouse. He stumbled and fell backwards, hitting his head against the toilet. He was killed instantly by the impact.

For the next hour, bits and pieces of the aliens crawled up out of the toilet and rolled in his fresh blood, absorbing its nutrients. Claws tore his body open so that the alien chunks could get inside and wallow in even more of his wholesome, nourishing gore.

- - -

Jacob Moretti spent two hours on the phone.

When he'd called 911, he was transferred from one operator to another and so on and so forth. He kept being put on hold for endless durations, during which he listened to tedious, preprogrammed Muzak. Finally the music stopped and a human voice piped up.

"Mr. Moretti?" the voice said.

"Yes, that's me," Jacob said sleepily, as he awoke from a Muzak-induced stupor.

"I'm Captain Morris Price from the NYPD. I hear you found a substantial amount of blood in your toilet. It's nothing to worry about. It's actually rat blood."

"*Rat* blood?" Jacob said. "I don't believe it. How could so much rat blood get into my toilet?"

"It was definitely a freak occurrence," Captain Price said. "Several hundred rats on the subway rails were hit by a train, and all their blood and gore flowed into a broken water pipe. I suggest you contact your maintenance man. He should be able to take care of the situation."

"That explanation doesn't make any sense at all," Jacob said. "If a water pipe is broken, water is going to pour *out*. Nothing is going to pour *in*. What is this, some kind of half-baked cover-up? I've been on hold for all this time, just to hear such ridiculous gibberish?" With that, he slammed down the phone.

Apparently his wife was right. He was going to have to call Max after all.

He picked up the phone once again.

- - -

Linnea Stevens in 9D grew worried as her brand-new dishwasher made a series of weird gurgling and bumping noises. It sounded more like a dilapidated antique than the state-of-the-art appliance she had purchased only two days earlier.

Dark-red, reeking gore began seeping out from around the edges of the dishwasher's door.

Linnea quickly turned off the machine.

The gurgling stopped, but the bumping continued.

"Maybe it's just a rat –" she whispered, trying desperately to convince herself that this was just a simple rodent problem. Deep down, she knew that it had to be something much worse.

Suddenly the door popped wide open.

The entire inside of the dishwasher was filled with ragged loops of intestines, drenched in rotten blood.

"Oh – oh nooooo –"

She pulled her cellphone out of her pocket, but didn't even get the chance to hit the 9 in 911. The intestines flew out of the machine and wrapped themselves around her body, her limbs – her throat. Then the intestines began to squeeze, tighter and tighter, until Linnea's eyes popped out of her now purpled face. Blood poured down from her sockets and onto the intestines, instilling the alien guts with fresh, murderous strength.

- - -

Max knocked on the front door of 2B.

He had a twenty-five-foot drain snake in one hand, his box of tools in the other, and his tool belt wrapped around his waist. When he heard about the blood in the toilet bowl, he figured it would be just a few drops of rusty water – the tenants were always prone to exaggeration. He would snake the drain and be out of there in time to catch the Giants game.

"Hey, Max. It's bad," Jacob said as he opened the door. "*Real* bad. If you need any help, just let me know."

"Thanks for the offer." Max entered the condo. "I should be able to handle this myself."

When the maintenance man saw all the blood – *actual* blood, not just rust-water – inside the toilet bowl, he grew nauseous. Then he heard a hollow voice from out of nowhere say, "Sludge lives –"

"What did you say, Mr. Moretti?" Max shouted.

"I didn't say anything." Jacob appeared at the door of the bathroom. "I have to tell ya, Max, you're looking a little green around the gills right now. Just like my wife. She just couldn't handle it. Right now, she's visiting a friend in 3C. Before she left, she said this blood must have something to do with voodoo. Do you think that's what's going on? Somebody running a voodoo cult here in the building?"

Max thought for a moment. "You know what? I'm not going to rule that out. New York's a weird city. Anything's possible." He started to unwind the snake and plunge it into the crimson sludge. "I've got this covered," he said. "You go watch some TV."

Jacob nodded and left.

Max spooled all twenty-five feet of line down the toilet drain, and still it would not unclog. That had never happened before in all his years of working as a maintenance man. He was starting to wind it back up when the line suddenly jerked, like a fishing line with an Atlantic blue marlin at the other end. He had to use all his strength to reel it back in.

"Damn," he said, breathing heavily. "Maybe those urban legends about alligators in the sewer are true –"

Just then, a sludge-streaked claw emerged from the bloody toilet water and grabbed Max by the wrist. He dropped to the floor, breaking his tool belt and causing the snake reel to fall to the ground.

The maintenance man struggled to his feet, grabbed the plunger, and beat at the claw until at last it let go of him.

"Jacob!" Max yelled.

"Yeah? What's going on?" The tenant ran into the bathroom. He saw the claw as it tried to grab at Max's pant-leg.

"Holy crap!" Jacob yelled.

"Hand me my wrench," Max said, batting at the claw with the plunger.

Jacob pulled the wrench out of the tool belt. "I'll give it a whack!" he cried, beating at the monster from the toilet. But on the fourth swing of the wrench he missed, cracking the porcelain and causing rotted blood to flood the floor. He kept whacking at the claw as hard as he could. The battered claw retreated down the toilet pipe.

The entire bathroom was splashed with rancid blood – on the floor, walls, bathtub and ceiling. But the alien claw was finally gone.

Both Max and Jacob stared down into the broken bowl.

"What the hell *was* that thing?" Jacob shouted.

"The hell if I know!" Max said. "Think we should call the police?"

"I called them earlier about the blood and they didn't do a thing. But if we called them and told them about *this*. They'd think we were having an LSD trip! They'd probably think we'd chopped up some bodies and flushed them down the toilet!" Jacob pointed a trembling finger at the broken toilet. "My wife was right. This is some kind of crazy-ass voodoo. Nobody is going to help us!"

"So we've got to fix this ourselves?"

"Yeah, I guess so. We've gotta fix it ourselves."

"How do we do *that*?"

"I have no idea."

- - -

Jacob and Max sat on the edge of the tub. They had finished the last beer in the twenty-four-pack. Besides stinking blood clots everywhere, there were also plenty of empty cans.

"I have an idea —" Jacob slurred out the words. "I own a warehouse that went out of business. Still trying to sell the building. We had some military contracts. For a while, some uniforms, bio-hazard suits, weapons, and other assorted items were stored there. When we went bankrupt, the military took most of their stuff back, but left behind a few things, like some of the bio-hazard suits, a few desks —and a black drum filled with fluoroantimonic acid. They needed to make special arrangements to transport it, and somewhere along the line, I guess they forgot. Either that or it's tied up in paperwork."

"So what's this fluoro-stuff?" Max asked. "Toothpaste?"

"Toothpaste? If you brushed your teeth with fluoroantimonic acid, you wouldn't have any teeth *left*. Hell, you wouldn't even have a *head* left! It's a super-acid, *very* corrosive!"

"Do you think it can melt that claw thing?"

"Hell yeah!" Jacob said, finishing the last swallow of his beer. "And if there are more claw things down there, it'll melt them, too. Did you ever see that movie, *Raiders of the Lost Ark*?"

"Yeah —"

"You know that scene where that German guy opens the Ark and his face melts off?"

"Yeah–"

"That's what fluoroantimonic acid does. It melts *everything*. Even glass and plastic! It can only be stored in a container lined with Teflon."

"Awesome!" Max cried. "That stuff will dissolve that voodoo claw-thing down to its atoms. But how are we going to get that stuff? I thought you said your warehouse went out of business."

"It sure did – but the building is still there and I have the keys. A pickup, too!" Jacob weaved a bit as he rose to his feet. "We'll put on those bio-hazard suits, to be on the safe side. Come on, let's go!"

- - -

Two hours later, Max and Jacob returned from the warehouse with a black drum emblazoned with yellow skull-and-crossbones symbols and the words HIGHLY CORROSIVE and TOXIC.

They used a dolly from the warehouse to haul the drum into the building. They wore some bio-hazard suits they found, and many tenants were alarmed when they saw the two dressed that way, hauling in a big black drum.

"Let's pour this stuff down a toilet on the top floor," Max said. "There's an empty unit up there, so the fumes won't bother anyone. It ought to dissolve any voodoo claws in its way as it pours down the pipes."

Carrying the drum up the stairs with the dolly seemed to take forever, but they had to do it that way because the brownstone condos had no elevator.

At last they reached the unit on the top floor. Max unlocked the door and together, they maneuvered the black drum into the bathroom.

"Here goes nothing!" Jacob cried as they poured the fluoroantimonic acid directly into the toilet.

As the corrosive fluid poured out of the drum, Max happened to notice a warning label covered with fine print on the side of the container.

The text on the label included the phrase: REACTS EXPLOSIVELY WITH WATER.

The resulting explosions filled the structure with corrosive gases, reducing Max, Jacob and all the other people inside to bubbling gore.

Everything dissolved in the path of the destructive fluids and fumes as they ate their way down, down, down to the sewers below.

Along the way, the alien sludge and all of its chunks, large and small, dissolved to nothing – and in the sewer, a hollow, dying voice managed to utter, "Sludge lives – no more –"

I originally wrote a novella about zombies taking over in the Quad Cities with "To Live & Die In IA: Zombies in Iowa" but it was just too long for this collection. I decided to write another tale for this book and the end result was little darker and weirder. A thanks goes out to Char for helping me with the research for this undead yarn set in my hometown —

RED SNOW
by Michael McCarty

It started with the cold front, bitterly frigid temperatures that swept all across the United States from north to south and east to west. Zero degrees, below zero degrees and with the wind chill factor even more wintry. And then the weird stuff started happening – the cold caused frozen iguanas to fall from trees in Florida, sharks and whales were washed up frozen in Georgia, frozen rats in Chicago and garter snakes frozen on the sidewalks in Portland.

Then came the snow. It snowed and snowed and snowed. It didn't seem like it was ever going to stop. Birds that migrated south for the winter were dying in droves. Orange and pineapple trees in California stopped bearing fruit.

And then all the snow turned red. The snowflakes that dropped from the sky were no longer white, but crimson. It looked like the sky was bleeding. People had all kinds of theories about it – red rain that froze, dust from Mars – but nobody had time to find out the real reason, because that was when the dead returned back to life again and feasted on the living –

Emma Erickson drove her Ford F-150 truck easily through the red snow. The roads in Rock Island, Illinois had been salted, but were still slick in spots, the F-150 plowed through the red frosty slush to Hilltop Dry Cleaners without sliding too badly. This was the best thing she had got from her ex. During bad weather it was great for getting around, but normally the vehicle was too much of a gas guzzler, sucking down the fuel

111

like a dehydrated vampire.

She was dreading going to work today, the red snow made business slower and because fellow worker, Susan O'Day, hadn't been at the cleaners for over a week, it meant she'd also have to fill in doing counter work as well. Nothing against working the front, but she didn't know what to say to customers anymore. Everybody seemed to take offense to even the most innocent of comment. It seemed society was going backward these days, not forward.

Emma was about half a block from work, when she started to slow down. Not because of the weather conditions but what she saw in the parking lot – a red truck attached to a thirty foot trailer also red, labeled with big block letters that read:

ROCK ISLAND FIRE DEPARTMENT:
HAZARDOUS MATERIALS

She pulled into the parking lot, stopped and dialed her boss Hannah. As the phone rang: "WTF?" "Why is a Haz Mat truck in front of work?" "Was it some kind of chemical spill?" "Is it safe to go inside?"

The questions remained unanswered, because Hannah's phone went straight to voicemail.

"This is Emma," she said to the voicemail. "I'm in the parking lot. Give me a call back as soon as possible and let me know what the hell is going on."

Looked at her watch. Fifteen minutes before work started.

Waited and waited and waited.

Looked at the watch once again. Five minutes before work started. Looked up at the truck again and gingerly inched past the Haz Mat her vehicle and pulled to the front of the cleaners, where Hannah's car was parked.

Next to her boss' car was Patty's Beetle. That was as strange as seeing both doors to the shop were wide open.

"Hannah!" Emma yelled, "Patty!" She walked through the front doors looking at the lobby, front counter, the backroom and in the open-door bathroom. She checked everywhere, including the boss' office. No sign of them whatsoever.

"That's strange," she whispered to herself.

She dialed Hannah again. Same result – voicemail. She called Patty next – voicemail too. Odd and even oddier.

Emma decided her boss might have gone to the Rock Island Fire Department and that was why her empty truck was there. Everyones vehicle was at work but nobody was there and how would they have all gotten o the Fire Department without any means of transportation?

She had many questions, but no answers.

There was still work to do. After working for the dry cleaners for the last two years she knew the drill:

Press.

Steam.

Iron.

Fold.

Package.

And start all over again.

She started up the pressing machine and waited for the steam to get hot. The machine was nicknamed "The Barbecue," because it got up to temperatures as hot as 600 degrees Fahrenheit.

There was a video camera recording the area where she pressed, because customers complained twice as much about lost clothing than damaged clothing, so her boss recorded everything and doubled down on the invoices to try to avoid this from happening.

She heard a slurping sound, like someone sucking on a spaghetti dinner or drinking to get the last few drops from their slushie.

"Hannah! Patty!" Still no answer.

She heard the slurping noise again. This time she listened and could tell it was coming from the backroom.

Emma went into the backroom and could hear lapping and guzzling from behind the steel door in the back. The back door hadn't been opened since she began working at the cleaners. Even on the hottest and most sultry days of summer it remained locked because the business wasn't in the best part of town and some other establishments had been robbed before.

She unlocked the door, and opened it and saw someone lying on the sidewalk in a puddle of blood and gore. Hannah was kneeling beside her, maybe applying bandages to the wound to stop it from bleeding anymore. Emma took a few steps out and saw that the person on the ground was her co-worker Patty, and that her boss was kneeling next not to the body not to help with first aid, but to eat bloody bits of flesh from her badly torn neck.

Hannah turned around and Emma saw that her face was covered in blood and gore and her eyes were milky white, no color in her pupils whatsoever.

Emma became nauseous, close to vomiting. She had seen enough zombie movies and TV shows to know that her boss was now one of the living dead.

She started to run back to the dry cleaners, but with all the snow on the ground, it was very slippery and she fell before reaching the door. When Emma was first hired, she had to watch a training video about the dangers of PERC (a chemical known as perchloroethylene or tetrachloroethylene). They hadn't had any instructions about when your boss turned into a flesh eating zombie and wanted to eat you.

Emma quickly got up, but her boss grabbed by her by the legs, dragging her back to the ground.

Hannah staggered towards her, like she had been on a weekend drinking binge. From the years that Emma took karate, she did her best side kick at her superior's right knee, as hard as she could.

It was successful because Hannah fell to the ground like a novice ice skater.

Emma quickly got up and ran back inside to the pressing machine to grab her purse and coat. It was too late. Her boss grabbed her by her hair, pulling her closer . She pulled her boss' hands out from her hair and pushed them onto the scalding surface of the pressing machine.

Hannah screamed in pain.

Emma grabbed her boss by the head and shoved her face on to the red-hot burning surface and brought the pressing machine together, searing her superior's face. She kept pushing down on the equipment, harder and harder, until she heard the skull crack.

Hannah's body, which was jerking around like a drunk frat boy just tazed by the police, then suddenly went flaccid.

She released the pressing machine and her boss' limp body fell to the floor.

Emma ran to her truck, grabbed the keys from her purse and was about to put the key in the keyhole when she felt an icy cold hand against the back of her shoulder. She turned around only to see Patty standing behind her. Like boss, she had become a zombie too. And her neck continued to bleed.

Emma's keys were still in her hand. She jabbed them into Patty's white eye. Soon the eye did turn a color, bloody red as blood spurted out of the open wound like a fountain.

When her co-worker put a hand on the cut to try to stop the bleeding, Emma used the opportunity to put the bloody key into the keyhole, open the door and with the last of energy she could muster, jumped into the truck and locked the door.

Emma started up the truck, shifted into drive and floored the pedal. The vehicle slid on the parking lot pavement towards the street. Before she pulled onto 18th Avenue, she saw three zombie firemen blocking her path, but that was only temporary as the truck rammed into the trilogy of the undead and they were quickly airborne, before crashing and landing on to the street. The whole scene looked like a horror movie about bowling a strike.

Emma didn't even bother looking to see if the zombie firemen were going to get back up or not, because the truck was speeding down 18th Avenue as she made her escape.

Shortly after Joe McKinney and I had our novella Lost Girl Of The Lake published by Bad Moon Book were invited to write for the anthology Before Plan 9: Plans 1-8 From Outer Space, edited by Tony Schaab, for TwinStar Media. The theme of Before Plan 9 is this: What were the other 8 plans before Plan 9 From Outer Space? Joe and I are both fans of Ed Wood. We had fun writing this…

Lost Girl of The Lake which was a Bram Stoker Finalist for "Superior Achievement in Long Fiction." Unfortunately the book didn't win, but was recently republished by Grinning Skull Press in 2018.

TERROR OF BRISTOL PLAINS
By Joe McKinney & Michael McCarty

"Because all you of Earth are stupid" – *Plan Nine From Outer Space*

"Perhaps, on your way home, someone will pass you in the dark, and you will never know it – for they will be from outer space" – *Plan Nine From Outer Space*

"You didn't like it? Well, my next one will be even better" – Ed Wood Jr.

1.

It was hot inside Dave Cunningham's '52 Ford. A West Texas desert breeze carried the scent of honeysuckle and jasmine in through the open windows. Margaret Summers leaned back against the passenger door; her heart pounding in her chest as Dave planted kisses along her throat. Things were happening fast. *Too fast.* She should stop this, she knew. Any farther and they'd be unable to resist where these urges – these *needs* – were taking them. But before she could tell him to stop, his hand slid under her blouse, and then under her bra, and she gasped.

"Dave," she said, his name hitching in her throat. He had her earlobe between his teeth now, his hand cupped over her breast. She could feel a damp heat spreading between her legs, and with it came a yearning that both shocked and overwhelmed her. She was a good girl. She was a good girl, and good girls don't –

"Dave," she said again, grabbing him by the wrist.

The tip of his tongue danced on the porch of her ear.

His hand retreated from her breast, and for a moment, she thought she was safe. But then his hand slid under the hem of her skirt and found her thigh; it moved dangerously upward from there.

She could barely breathe.

"Dave!" she gasped, her head spinning. Her eyes were wide open now, but all she could see was his black hair, and her fingers grabbing hungrily at his shirt.

Margaret turned her head, and caught a glimpse of what was going on in the backseat. Mel Pournelle was on top of Jeannie Potts; his hand was so far up her thigh that Margaret could see the top of her best friend's stockings. Jeannie's mouth was open, her breasts heaving. Mel was pulling her blouse from her skirt, pushing it up over Jeannie's stomach the flesh white in the moonlight.

That was enough for Margaret.

She pushed Dave's massive shoulders away with all the strength she could muster.

He stared back at her, hungry-looking and confused.

"Are you okay?" he asked.

"Not here," she whispered. She could barely catch her breath. "Please."

He blinked. She could feel him, hard as a diamond drill against her leg, and at that moment Margaret knew this was it. It was going to happen tonight. Jeannie had already done it; as Margaret laid there with her hands on Dave's shoulders, she briefly thought about how Jeannie had described it. She said it hurt like a son-of-a-gun the first time, but then it got really good after that, like fireworks going off inside you.

"Where?" he asked.

"On the hill," she said. "Under the stars."

He looked at her then, and the moon shining in his eyes was all the proof she needed. He was the one, and this was the time. She was ready.

They both reached for the door handle at the same time.

The next instant they were running hand in hand across the grassy knoll that overlooked the old Kellman Army Air Base. From here, they could look over the ruins of what the military had left behind, row upon row of empty, crumbling barracks, and further on, the hangars where B-17s had fueled on their way to Europe and the Pacific.

Margaret saw all of this, and none of it. Dave was working open the buttons on her blouse. She let it come off. The next instant, her bra slid off her shoulders. Instinctively, she put a hand across her chest to cover herself, but he gently guided her arm away and laid her out on the gently sloping hillside. She felt like her shoulders had been pinioned to the grass, and when Dave peeled off his shirt, Margaret thought her heart would pound its way out of her ribcage.

She smiled up at him. But the smile faded to a look of rapt fascination and naked lust as he unbuttoned the waist of her skirt.

"Are you sure you're ready?" he asked.

She nodded. It was all she could do: Margaret wanted to be cool, and graceful, and beautiful. She wanted to be Elizabeth Taylor. But instead, she was so scared she could hardly speak.

He tugged at the waist of her skirt, trying to work it down over her hips. She lifted herself just, enough to let him, and suddenly the sky filled with light.

Margaret screamed.

A police car, she thought. They were busted for sure. Her Dad was going to kill her.

But then the light moved off. She looked up at Dave, who was on his knees between her legs, looking up at the sky. The lights she had seen were moving off, over the base.

She sat up, arms crossed over her breasts. "What is that?"

Dave shook his head, but didn't answer.

"Dave?"

He stammered incomprehensibly.

It was some kind of plane, she thought. *It had to be.* But it was unlike any plane she'd ever seen. It reminded her more of a gargantuan child's top with orange and red fire glowing from the bottom of the craft. The plane

– if that was indeed what it was, though she already doubted that – was putting out a huge amount of explosive power. And yet, oddly, it made very little noise as it glided over the barracks. It moved with an effortless grace, more like a ship at sea than a plane in the sky, and Margaret, despite her fear, watched in amazement.

She didn't look away until Dave managed to stagger to his feet. He was backing away from the sight, shielding his eyes from the lights.

Margaret grabbed her clothes and ran to him.

The two of them stood on the hillside overlooking the base and watched as the ship glided down to the main hangar on the other side of the barracks and disappeared inside. For a moment, the hangar looked like it was on fire, lights shooting out from every window, every crack, and every door. And then, just as suddenly as the craft appeared above their heads, the lights went out. An eerie, silent darkness dropped over the base once more.

"Oh my God," Dave said.

"I thought the military abandoned this place," Margaret said.

"That wasn't a military plane," Dave said.

She looked at him. "What then?"

"We don't have anything like that in our military."

"The Russians?" she asked.

"Them either."

That stopped her. Dave knew about these things. He was the quarterback for the Parker High School Cougars, but he wasn't just a dumb jock. He had plans to go to the Naval Academy and fly fighters. Maybe even become an astronaut one day. If he said there was nothing like this on Earth –

"Dave, I want to leave here."

"Yeah," he said, swallowing hard. "Yeah, I agree."

2.

"You were WHERE?" Sheriff Jack Summers stared at his daughter – his daughter, for Christ's sake! – in horrified disbelief. Good God, what was the world coming to? One minute, she was his little angel, his giggling little girl in pigtails, and the next, she was up on the hills above the old Kellman Army Air Base. Kids only went out there for *one* reason.

Slowly, his anger mounting, he turned his attention on Dave Cunningham. The boy was the Cougar's star quarterback and class president, probably going to be the valedictorian too. Talk around town was that he'd already been accepted to Annapolis. He was a local celebrity. But if he had put one greasy paw on Margaret, Jack wanted to make it very clear that he was going to be a *dead* local celebrity.

"Daddy," Margaret said, "please listen. We saw this thing coming out –"

"Young lady, the best thing you can do right now is shut your mouth."

"Daddy, we –"

"Shut it. Go to your room."

"Daddy –"

"Now!"

Margaret's lips were trembling. She looked to her mother for support, got none, and ran sobbing up the stairs.

A moment later, a door slammed.

Jeannie Potts was trying to melt into the wallpaper. Jack had known her since she was four years old, when she and her folks moved to Bristol Plains, and frankly he had expected better of her. He had expected better of all of them.

But he turned his tone down a notch for her. "Jeannie, will you go sit in the kitchen, please? I'm going to call a patrol car to take you home."

The girl nodded without looking up and hurried into the kitchen.

That left the two boys. Jack turned on Dave and the other boy, Mel Pournelle. Mel took a few steps back. But Dave didn't move. He lifted his chin and met Jack in the eye.

As much as Jack wanted to punch the boy's lights out, he did have to admit the kid had a backbone. That said something for him.

"She was telling you the truth," Dave said. "We saw some really wild lights in the sky. And something went into the main hangar down there. I think it was a spaceship, sir."

Jack regarded him coldly. "You smoke reefer, son?"

"No sir."

"You drunk?"

"I'm not drunk either, sir. I saw what I saw."

"A spaceship?"

"I've spent the last three years studying every plane in every military on the planet, sir. What we saw tonight was a spaceship. Nobody on Earth flies anything like it."

Jack nodded. He had heard enough.

"I'll tell you what. You and Mel, you get in your car and go home. I mean it, you go home. And if you're smart, you don't say a word about this foolishness to anybody, you hear? From what I know, you got a future. But if you go around telling people about Martians coming to Bristol Plains, that future's gonna dry up real fast."

Mel took a tentative step forward and gave Dave a nudge. "Hey Dave, let's take off. What do you say? That's good advice."

Dave shook off his friend's hand.

"I saw what I saw, sir."

"Fine," Jack said. "Fine. Here's how this is gonna work. I got a shotgun in the next room loaded down with rock salt. If you and your friend here ain't gone by the time I come back with it, I'm gonna pepper both your butts. And if I ever I catch you within one hundred feet of my daughter, I swear to God you're gonna be missin' a pecker. You hear me, son?"

"Yes sir," said Dave. "I hear you just fine. Come on, Mel, let's go get a Coke down at the Allende."

The next instant, the boys were gone, Dave's Ford spitting gravel out behind it as it raced away down Blue Stem Road.

Jack stood there in the middle of the living room, fuming mad. He heard Linda, his wife, behind him. She was clicking her tongue against the roof of her mouth. It was an annoying habit, one she did whenever she was about to nag him for whatever he'd done.

"Congratulations," she said to his back. "You've managed to completely alienate your daughter. You must be very proud."

"Don't you start with me."

"Oh, I wouldn't dream of it."

"Dammit, Linda, she's seventeen. She has no business going out to Kellman with a boy. You know damn well what happens out there."

"I do indeed," his wife said. "I remember it quite fondly, in fact."

Jack sighed. *Damn woman, she always did know how to take the wind out of my sails.* "She's a baby," he said.

"She's in love with that boy."

"She's seventeen! What in the hell does she know about love?"

"I seem to remember we had a pretty good handle on things at that age. And on each other."

"Yeah, I remember. That's the part that's got me upset."

She crossed the living room and kissed his chin. She brushed her fingertips around the curve of his ear, down the strong, square line of his jaw. He was forty-one, his muscles still hard, his belly still flat, still every bit as handsome as the boy she'd fallen in love with before the war. But sometime in between, webs of worry lines had formed at the corner of his eyes. The man had so much on his mind.

"Go easy on her," Linda said. "You can't fight love. All you'll end up doing is driving her straight into his arms."

He nodded. His brown eyes looked sad, tired.

"I need to call a car to take Jeannie home."

"You do that," she said. "Just do me a favor, okay?"

"What's that?"

"Try to remember what seventeen was like." She winked impishly. "And if you think you can do that, I'll wait up for you tonight."

"Ah –" he said, and a smile tugged at the corners of his mouth.

She went upstairs to talk to Margaret, leaving him alone in the living room. He called Jolene Grissom, his dispatcher, and asked her to send a car over. Wes Givens was on duty tonight. The young deputy was a little thick sometimes, but he could be trusted to follow directions to the letter, and he wasn't prone to exaggeration. He'd do for what Jack had in mind.

It was that old base that had him worried. Not the Martians Margaret had been babbling on about. That was just kid stuff. Too many of them damn monster movies down at the Allende Drive-In.

No, Jack's concerns ran deeper than that.

He had a history with that base.

Kellman was shut down for a while after World War I. But then it was brought back in the late 1930s as a research installation for white scientists and a training base for black soldiers. But even then, up to the start of

World War II, it was largely abandoned. It was certainly empty enough that he and Linda had been able to enjoy more than a few quiet nights under the stars out there.

Then, when Jack came home from his own war in the Pacific in the '40s, he'd joined up with the Parker County Sheriff's Office under Sheriff Ben Scott. One of his first calls had been out to the base to help clean up after a disaster in one of the barracks.

He was told it was a gas leak.

And though Jack could smell the faint hint of gas in the air, he didn't believe it for a second. He'd fought on fourteen islands in the Pacific Campaign, and seen men killed in all sorts of horrible ways.

None of them compared to what he saw in those barracks.

Gauzy webs hung from the ends of beds, the windowsills, the doorways, and the roof rafters. Thirty-two black soldiers lay in twisted piles on the ground, swollen red welts all over their arms and faces, their clothes torn to ribbons, like the men had tried to tear them off in desperation. Their faces were frozen in expressions of such horror that Jack nearly lost his nerve and ran out.

While he was helping to drag the bodies outside, he heard two of the scientists talking about spiders. Thinking of the webs inside, he paused and listened. The scientists had only been in earshot for a few moments, but what he heard frightened him to the core. The scientists had raised some kind of killer spiders in their labs, and those spiders had gotten loose inside these barracks, killing the soldiers. The scientists had gassed the barracks, which killed the spiders, but they weren't sure if they'd gotten them all. That last part had made Jack's skin crawl.

Over the next few months, the military covered up the deaths of the thirty-two black soldiers. Jack imagined that part hadn't been hard to do, not the way blacks were treated. And when the base closed for good in '46, the event was almost entirely forgotten. The few men still alive who had been in those barracks with Jack hadn't thought anything of it, just a bunch of dead black men. No big loss at least as far as most white men of the day were concerned.

But Jack never forgot the way that scientist had trembled when they admitted they didn't know if they'd gotten them all.

And now his daughter had been out there at that base, above those barracks.

The things that could have happened.

Why, he wondered, *are fathers cursed to dream up such terrible fates for their children?*

3.

Space Commander Eros was not happy. His trip back to the home world had been unexpected and unpleasant. And it could not have come at a more inopportune time, now that his most recent Plan was in such a critical phase.

But what was he to do?

Politics could be a deadly game. Immediately after landing on the home world he realized that there was a new power play at work. The Ruler had been his usual self: friendly, kind, and generous. His Excellency often made the trip between the home world and the various Space Stations, but rarely did he recall his Commanders, especially his Space Commanders when they were in mid-implementation of a Plan. Upon his arrival, Eros quickly discovered that The Ruler was not the problem.

The problem was Sector Commander Agar.

Agar was a ruthless politician. He had no family, no obligations but to the job, and he was consumed by his ambition. That, in and of itself, was nothing new. Eros had faced power-hungry opponents like that throughout his long career. What made Agar different was that he was smart. He was not just a politician, but a master at logistics as well. He had done Eros' job not too long ago, implementing a successful Plan in the Gall Sevus quadrant.

Agar definitely had the background and the training to run an expeditionary force and that was why The Ruler put him in this newly-created administrative position. No longer would Eros report directly to The Ruler. From here on out, Agar would be the watchdog, the bureaucrat second-guessing Eros' every move. It made Eros furious, and not just because he'd lost face in front of the High Council. No, he was furious because Agar was gifted. He wasn't just another coin counter; like Eros, he was thoroughly versed on the history of the Earth and their people's expeditions there throughout history, and he knew Eros' operations (and recent failures) in the minutest detail. And, of course, he did not waste time questioning Eros in front of The Ruler and the High Council. He had insinuated that, because Eros was so talented, he might be over-thinking his Plans and that he was starting to slip.

That was the real reason Eros was so angry. He was angry at himself, for letting things get to this point to begin with. It had been a rough five hours in front of the High Council, beating himself up like that.

But the ignominy of Agar's interrogation wasn't the worst. The real insult had been the removal of Tanna as his Subcommander. Agar had pointed out Eros' feelings for the young lieutenant, and he claimed this had clouded Eros' judgment.

Eros had protested that. Protested it quite vigorously, in fact, but his objections were hollow. He knew that even as he'd said them.

Once again, Agar had proven himself right.

Afterwards, Eros had felt a bit rattled by it all.

But all the bitterness and anxiety his trip back home had caused was soon forgotten. He had far bigger problems.

His experiment was gone.

The first thing he had done upon his return was to begin the implementation of his next Plan – rather, what Agar had termed the "second phase" of his previous Plan. *Bureaucracy verbiage at its finest,* Eros thought glumly. He thought for sure that his previous Plan – the usage of the Enlarging Ray on Earth's lower life forms would be a sure-fire success. In retrospect the scope had been too broad. Using multiple species had weakened his ability to properly concentrate the Plan; he needed to focus on one specific animal, employ its strengths, and exploit the Earthlings' weaknesses.

This is what he planned to do with on the scytodes.

Ironically enough, it was the humans that planted the seeds of their destruction. They originated breeding experiments on the scytodes –what the humans called "ogre-eyed spitter spiders" – developing spiders that were far more lethal than any found in nature. Eros managed to track down the few specimens left behind when the humans abandoned the

126

base, and he cultivated them. He tweaked their DNA and produced the perfect *killing* machine. They had lost their ability to spit their poison, but that poison was now far more dangerous, and they had grown razor-sharp vampire fangs to inject it into their victims.

But the enhanced fangs were just the beginning, for Eros had gone far beyond simple genetic selection strategies to enhance the potency of their poison. Using the Enlarging Ray, he had grown the spiders to enormous size. The adult specimens were as big as the automobiles the Earthlings used to move around. And any human unlucky enough to cross paths with one of his spiders would have far more to worry about than a simple scratch. The full-sized specimens marked the pinnacle of his work. And because they were so large, he had little trouble containing them. However, the smaller specimens, the babies posed, that posed the bigger problem.

Mainly because they were gone.

After returning to the base, he'd gone straight for their tanks, only to find them empty. The lead-lined curtain he'd draped over the top of the tanks had a weight-to-mass ratio that should have kept the spiders safely contained. By his calculations, it would have taken eighteen spiders, working in tandem, to move that kind of mass, so he felt safe in leaving a single spider in each tank. But they had managed to move both the curtains and the lids just the same. And now here he was, facing a nightmare.

If word of this got back to home world, they'd relieve him of command immediately.

Agar would probably take personal satisfaction in it, in fact.

Just then, the Televisor buzzed.

Not now, Eros thought. Please don't be him.

But it was. Eros crossed the floor to the Televisor and activated the picture. When Agar's image wavered into view, Eros felt his entire body tense.

"Yes, sir?" Eros said.

"By my calculations, you should have returned to Earth approximately seventeen minutes ago. Is this correct?"

"Yes, Sector Commander. I am here."

"And your experiment? Report on your readiness status of the next phase of your Plan?"

My status, Eros thought bitterly. *Somewhere between utter humiliation and career suicide, I'd estimate.*

But what he said was: "All is well. I will be ready for the next phase."

"That is in three days," Agar said. "Are you sure?"

Eros couldn't help but picture what would happen if the Earthlings spotted the infant spiders. They would easily destroy them. And, of course, knowing the humans as he did, they would study the specimens.

That would destroy all his plans. They'd be ready for him then.

"Eros? Is everything okay?"

"Everything is fine," Eros said. "When the moment comes, I'll be ready."

4.

As he drove the Potts girl back home, Deputy Wayne Givens couldn't help but steal a glance now and then at her chest. The girl was definitely built for fun. And if the gossip his kid sister Adeline told him was even half right, she wasn't afraid to let those big melons of hers come out and play every once in a while.

Wayne sighed. *Why didn't they have girls like that when he was in high school? What a shame.*

Of course, Jeannie Potts didn't seem like she'd be up for putting out anytime soon. The girl looked like she was in shellshock. Maybe she and the others were telling the truth about seeing something out there at Kellman. Wayne didn't really believe in Martians, not like in the movies anyway, but he had seen things out that way too. He'd seen weird lights, moving low and fast across the desert. He'd heard weird shrieking noises on the wind –

"This is my street here," said the girl.

Her voice caught Wayne by surprise.

"Huh?"

"Right up here. Myrtle Street. I'm the third house down on the left."

"Got it." Wayne turned onto her street and guided his patrol car down to the house she'd indicated. He reached to turn the ignition off, but she stopped him.

"You don't – have to tell my parents, do you?"

"Well–"

"Please," she said, and when she turned in the seat to face him, that chest of hers rose; like twin moons over the desert.

Wayne swallowed the lump that had suddenly formed in his throat. The inside of the car was uncomfortably stuffy and hot. Was she coming on to him? He couldn't tell. Not exactly, anyway. He wiped the back of his hand across his lips, thinking about her breasts in his hands.

Then: *Christ, what am I doing? What the hell's wrong with me? I got orders, for Christ's sake.*

Sheriff Summers' instructions had been perfectly clear on the matter. He was to take the girl home, tell her parents what she'd been up to, and then go check out the old Kellman Army Air Base to see if there was anything at all to the kids' story. And that was exactly what he was going to do.

Wayne looked over at her with every intention of telling her *sorry, but things have to be this way.* Unfortunately, right then, his gaze happened to stray downward to that amazing chest of hers, and he swallowed again. He quickly looked away, only to catch a surprising look in her eyes. The come-on he'd thought he'd seen just seconds ago looked more like fear right now. The girl, he realized, was terrified. Not of him, but of what he was going to tell her parents. Caught somewhere between being turned on by her shapely curves and moved to mercy by the humiliation she would no doubt suffer if he followed through on Sheriff Summers' instructions, his resolve wavered.

"Please," she begged, the tears threatening at the corners of her eyes. "My folks, they'll just kill me."

"Well, I suppose–"

"Thanks!" Jeannie said, suddenly brightening. "Goodnight!"

The next instant she was out of the car, running in those funny straight-armed way girls have up to her front porch, and disappeared inside. Wayne sighed and pulled away from the curb; he couldn't help but wonder if he'd just been played.

Maybe, he thought bitterly, *it was a good thing after all they didn't have girls like that back when I was in high school.*

5.

The Allende Drive-In was playing a special Bela Lugosi double-feature to memorialize the actor's death one year ago. *White Zombie* and *Dracula*. There was another double feature planned for Saturday, something about a wolfman and *Zombies on Broadway*. But to Dave Cunningham, it seemed like overkill. Lugosi was cool, he supposed, if you were into horror movies. But that wasn't his deal.

Dave was more into John Wayne. Especially his pilot movies like *The High and the Mighty* and *The Flying Leathernecks*. Now those were cool.

And besides, his failed date had been enough of a horror show for one night. He shook his head, thinking about the way Margaret had lifted her hips just enough for him to work her skirt down over them. God, he'd been so close. Waiting in line with Mel at the Allende's concession stand, Dave couldn't get the memory of Margaret's naked body out of his head. She was going to let him do it. He was certain that they were headed in that direction. He had seen it in her eyes, heard it in her breathing–

And then those damn lights had appeared overhead.

Dave took a deep breath. What, exactly, had they seen out there at Kellman? He'd been so certain that he'd seen a spaceship, an alien spaceship, but now that he was standing here at the drive-in, surrounded by cheesy monster movies and giggling kids, he wasn't so sure. Maybe Margaret's dad was right. Spaceships on Earth – the idea was ludicrous. And besides, why would aliens come all the way across the galaxy just to visit west Texas? They'd want to go to New York, or Washington, or Los Angeles, cool places like that. Wouldn't they?

"Hey, so you didn't tell me," Mel said as he gave Dave a playful slap on the shoulder. "How far did you get?"

"Huh?"

Mel smiled mischievously. "Don't play dumb. Dish it, man. Come on, how far did you get? You guys looked pretty hot and heavy before you took off."

Out of the corner of his eye, Dave saw a couple of sophomore girls in line in front of them. Adeline Givens and Ruth Ann Bass, both gossip queens extraordinaire. He could tell they were listening, trying to catch every word of the conversation. Anything they heard would be all over the school by Monday morning, and he didn't want that. Margaret Summers deserved better than that.

"I don't know what you're talking about, Mel. We just talked."

Mel gaped at him.

"Really, we just talked. That's all."

Adeline and Ruth Ann seemed to visibly deflate with disappointment. They turned back to the counter, ordered their drinks, and went off, whispering and giggling to each other. They probably didn't believe him, and Mel certainly didn't, but screw 'em all. It was none of their business.

Dave stepped up to the window.

"Hey guys," said the man at the register, "what can I get you?"

"Hey, Mr. Wheeler," Dave said. "Two Cokes, please."

Curtis Wheeler was Bristol Plains' one and only certifiable war hero. He'd earned two Silver Stars, a Bronze Star, and three Purple Hearts during the island fighting in the Pacific, and he'd even been mentioned in the United States Marine Corps' official history of World War II. Of course, he'd developed a bit of a gut since his soldiering days, but he was still a powerful-looking man, even in his white concession stand uniform and apron. A nice guy, too. He'd written a really good letter of recommendation for Dave back when Dave was trying to get Senator Gould to approve his bid for the Naval Academy.

"How's practice going?" Wheeler said, handing them their drinks. "You guys gonna have a good crew this year?"

"I think so," Dave said. He looked at Mel and Mel nodded. "We've got most of our backfield back this year. Our line's a little young, but they seem to be picking up the routine pretty quick. I think it'll be a good season for us."

Wheeler nodded. "Wish you had Carlton and Meyers back. Watching you throw the football to those two was something to behold."

"Thanks, Mr. Wheeler, that's —"

But Dave stopped mid-sentence. He'd caught a glimpse of something moving in the sink.

"What is that?" he asked. "Is that a spider?"

It was. A big one, too. It scurried up the sides of the basin, over the backsplash, and up the wall. The three of them stood there watching it, fascinated. It was huge, even for a desert spider. It had to be three inches long, easy.

The spider kept scurrying along the ceiling, moving quickly towards the light bulb over Wheeler's head.

"What the hell –?" Wheeler said.

The spider was a dusky gray with curling black veins along its back. But it was the face that didn't look right. It had enormous black eyes with blood red slits down the middle, and beneath the eyes, two enormous, hairy fangs.

"Oh God," Mel said. "That doesn't look like any spider I ever saw."

"I think that's one of them ogre-eyed spitting spiders," Wheeler said. "I saw one of them years ago, out by Kellman –"

He was still staring at the thing when Mel slapped Dave's shoulder.

"What is – ?" Dave started to say, but stopped. Mel's eyes were bugging out of his head, his mouth hanging open. He was backing away from the concession stand, pointing at the sink.

Dave looked that way, and gasped.

Hundreds of spiders, just like the one on the ceiling, were pouring out of the drain, crawling up the sides of the basin, climbing the walls, the popcorn machine, the floors –

"Mr. Wheeler, look out!" Dave shouted.

Wheeler had already seen them, but it was too late. The spiders kept coming, and within seconds they were all over everything. Wheeler was flailing away at the air, trying desperately to get them off, but there were just too many.

Screaming in pain, Wheeler fell against the far wall, near the deep fryers.

Dave backed away, watching in horror as Wheeler pulled a basket out of the boiling grease and swung it like a tennis racket at his attackers, even as the spiders climbed up his arms and onto his face.

Grease was flying everywhere. Some of it hit the electrical outlets behind the hot dog carousel, and the outlets erupted in a shower of sparks and angry popping sounds.

The next instant the sparks turned to flames that quickly climbed the wall.

Dave and Mel were still backing away, still too shocked to run.

As they stood there watching, Wheeler crashed against the counter's window, groaning horribly, his face shredded and bleeding, and then sagged down to the floor.

"Dave, what do we do?"

Just then the fire surged upward with an audible whoosh, sending out a wave of heat that caused both Dave and Mel to put hands in front of their faces.

"Dave?"

Dave just shook his head. Wheeler was dead. He knew he was supposed to do something, put the fire out or something, but all his brain could do was repeat the same refrain over and over again.

Wheeler was dead.

Mr. Wheeler was dead —

6.

The Kellman Army Air Base was just west of town, out on Highway 22. Wayne made it there in about twenty minutes. He didn't bother going to the main gates; when the base closed, the Army put large blocks of concrete across the roadway, ensuring that no vehicles could get inside. Everyone in town knew that if you wanted to see the base, you had to go up one of the service roads that skirted around the perimeter. More often times than not, that meant the north road that led up to the barracks' side of the base, where you could sit out on the hillside and watch the stars wheel over the desert. If Sheriff Summers' daughter and her friend with the big old melons had been out here with boys that was the way they almost certainly would have gone. And so that was the way he went.

He came to a stop on the hill above the barracks and stared out the windshield. The entire base was a dark and desolate ruin – except for the main hangar. The large front doors were open, and a blue light spilled out across the tarmac.

"What the hell?"

For a moment he debated backtracking to Bill Watson's Texaco station back on Highway 22 to call this in, but he quickly changed his mind. What would he say anyway? He had a suspicious light coming from a deserted base in the middle of nowhere. It could be anything in there. But, more than likely, it was nothing. Kids fixing up their cars, probably, getting ready to drag race out on the runway.

Still, he reached into the back seat for his shotgun and started walking down the hill. From the hillside, the base looked pristine in its desolation, but it was something else up close. Most of the barracks had holes in their roofs. Nearly every window was broken. Weeds had grown up along the baseboards and through the cracks in the concrete.

But what surprised Wayne most was the huge profusion of cobwebs.

They were everywhere, thick as curtains in places. They gave the place a creepy look, like that castle in Bela Lugosi's *Dracula*.

I don't want to be here, he thought.

By the time he cleared the last of the barracks and walked over towards the open hangar doors, he was certain something was wrong here. He wasn't sure what, but the beat-cop instincts in him were blaring warning signs in his brain.

He found out a moment later that his instincts were right.

Inside the hangar he saw an enormous – thing. He didn't know what else to call it; a spaceship, maybe. Yeah, that had to be it. The thing was saucer-shaped, but with a central collection of crystalline structures sticking out of the top that reminded him of something out of *The Wizard of Oz*. It was bizarre.

But the rest of the place was even stranger.

The saucer sat in the foreground. Behind it, all around it, were cages. At least that's what they looked like. They were made of some kind of shimmering, moving material, like soap bubbles. There were thousands of them. They hung from the ceilings and from the walls. They were stacked five or six deep on the floor, too. And inside each cage was a spider. A huge, sleeping spider. It was like nothing he had ever seen before.

The scene grew stranger still, for in the middle of those cages was some kind of control panel. It reminded Wayne of the bridge of a spaceship in a science-fiction movie.

A man was moving around in the middle of those control panels. He was dressed in a strange, shimmering bodysuit, almost like some sort of military flight suit, but definitely not like any he'd ever seen in the military.

Wayne let out a gasp.

The man at the controls suddenly spun around. His face thin, dignified, like one of those European intellectuals they showed in the movies sometimes. The man picked up a glowing metal tube about eight inches long and pointed it at the soap bubble cages behind him. Then he pressed a button and the rod began to hum.

Uh oh, Wayne thought.

He turned to run, but even as he sprinted out into the desert night, he knew he was too late. The bubble cages along the walls and hanging from the ceiling were popping, making a sound like a roomful of kids popping their bubblegum at all once. And when he looked back, he saw spiders dropping from the ceiling.

No, he thought, *not this way. Please.*

The deputy sprinted into the night. The barracks were just a few steps ahead, and for a moment he thought he might be able to hide there. Those things were so big, surely they wouldn't be able to make it through the doors or the windows.

But then, one of the spiders landed on the roof of the barracks in front of him. Things were happening in slow motion now. He could actually see the thing's legs bend and flex as it landed on the roof and then dropped to the ground in front of him.

"No," he said, shaking his head. "No."

He backed away.

And when he turned to look behind, he froze.

They were back there too. Coming closer. He was surrounded. How was this possible, he thought. He couldn't die. He wasn't supposed to. Not like this.

Not like this.

Dear God, no. Not like this.

7.

Jack rubbed the heel of his hand against his forehead, trying to head off the headache he knew was coming.

This easily ranked as the worst night of his life. First, his daughter tells him she's been up at the local make-out spot with her boyfriend, (and oh yes, he had recognized the look in that boy's eyes), followed by the Allende Drive-In burning down and killing one of the town's most respected citizens. And now, to top it all off, he had a missing deputy.

"Sheriff," said Jolene the dispatcher, "you still there?"

Jack put the phone back to his ear. "Yeah, Jolene, I'm here. Get Lieutenant Holson to head things up at the Allende. Tell him I'll contact him there in about an hour."

"Are you going out to Kellman?"

"Yeah, I'm gonna have to."

"There are a lot of parents out at the Allende, Jack. My phone's been ringing off the hook. They're asking questions I don't know how to answer."

"I know, Jolene. Just do the best you can, okay? I'll be there soon."

"Jack –"

"Yeah?"

"Do you think Wayne's okay?"

"I think so. Just hang on, Jolene. I'll get back with you as soon as I know something."

Jack hung up the phone and went back to rubbing his forehead. He could almost picture the scene out at the Allende Drive-In. It was Saturday night. Nearly every teenager in Parker County would be there. And with the flames visible for miles around, nearly every parent would be out there too.

Hopefully the Cunningham boy would have enough sense not to mention the spiders he'd seen attacking Curtis Wheeler right before the fire got out of control.

Somehow he doubted it, though.

Still, it was the Cunningham boy's description of the spiders that prompted Jack to check out the old Kellman Army Air Base first. They called to mind his own experience of cleaning up the bodies of those black servicemen all those years ago. And then there was Margaret's description of the weird lights she'd seen out there…

He went to the closet and grabbed his shotgun. Linda leaned against the wall next to him and watched as he loaded the weapon.

"What are you gonna do, Jack?"

"I'm gonna go out to Kellman and see if I can find Wayne Givens."

"Do you have any idea what's going on?"

He shook his head. "No, not yet. But whatever it is, that Kellman Base is the center of it. That much I'm sure of."

"You'll be careful?"

He put the shotgun down and took her in his arms. "Aren't I always," he said, and brushed the hair from her eyes.

Upstairs, Margaret sat at her desk, leaning towards the vent on her wall. When her parents talked in the living room, she could hear every word through that vent, and the things she'd heard tonight terrified her. The Allende was burning, and Curtis Wheeler was dead. And worse, Dave had been there. She'd said a prayer for him as soon as she heard, hoping that he wasn't in the thick of things, but she knew that was a long shot. Knowing Dave, he'd be neck-deep in trouble.

She took out her journal and turned to a clean page. If ever there was a night to put down on paper, it was this one. Nearly losing her virginity; a UFO; the Allende burning down and its owner dead; it'd been a wild night for sure.

But she couldn't bring herself to write. She was too angry with her father. She thinking about the way he'd ordered her off to her room, like she was still some eight-year-old kid; it made her furious all over again. He wouldn't even listen to her! Sometimes the man could be so bull-headed and mean. She could still see the look on his face when she told him she'd been out at the Kellman Base with Dave. That was really what made her mad, even more than being sent to her room.

She was a good girl. She was smart. And more importantly, she was in love with Dave. It wasn't wrong when you were in love. Her own mother had said as much - she'd heard that through the vent as well. And yet the look on her father's face had been one of complete disappointment and dawning horror. He was too much of a gentleman to ever use the word, but she knew he was thinking it. He was raising a tramp.

She slammed her fist down on her desk. She wasn't a tramp. She wasn't. She was a good girl, damn it.

Margaret sat staring at the blank page in front of her. There was so much emotion in her right now, and yet she couldn't make it come out on the page. It was maddening.

Her train of thought was broken by a sudden noise outside. The Richardson's dog barked.

A twig snapped – and it sounded like it was coming from right below her window!

Margaret closed her journal and pushed it underneath a magazine. Swallowing the lump in her throat, she went to the window and pulled the curtains back just enough for her to see out.

It was Dave. All at once her anger was gone and she was beaming. She looked back toward her closed door, then, as quietly as she could, raised the window.

"Dave," she said in a stage whisper.

He looked up.

"Hey," he said.

"Hey yourself. What are you doing here?"

"I have to come up. I have to talk to you."

"Are you crazy?" she said. "My Mom'll hear you."

"Margaret, please."

Something in his tone made the smile melt away from her face. "Okay," she said. "But be quiet."

He scaled the Spanish Oak outside her window with amazing ease. Watching him, she felt her lips moisten in anticipation. He was so strong, so graceful.

"Hey," he said, dropping down onto her windowsill.

"Hey," she said, and leaned forward to kiss him.

He kissed her back, but it was only a peck on her lips. She opened her eyes and studied him. He was nervous, jittery, not at all like his normal self. "What's wrong? Is it what happened at the Allende?" she asked.

He looked surprised. "You heard about that?"

"The vent," she said. "I heard my parents talking."

"Oh." He was quiet for a moment, and then he told her what he'd seen. All of it. And by the time he was done, she was trembling.

"We have to go out there," he said.

"What? Are you crazy?"

"No, I'm not. I've got my dad's camera in the car. We can get proof of what's out there, Margaret. None of them believe us, but if we can get proof, if we can really show them what we saw, maybe people like your dad can take action before it's too late."

He waited for a beat.

"What do you say? Will you come with me?"

"What? Now?"

"Yes, now," he said, laughing. Then the sudden smile that had lit his face disappeared. "It's up to us, Margaret. We're the only ones who can do this."

She looked into his eyes, and at that moment, she was lost. She'd been ready to give him her virginity earlier that evening. Her feelings hadn't changed. If anything, they'd grown stronger. They were welling up inside her, filling her heart so completely she felt like she might burst. She could lose herself in this man. He was so confident, so self-assured. He honestly believed he could save the world. And he wanted her at his side when he did it.

"I love you," she blurted out.

For a terrifying moment she stood there, her eyes full of shock at what she'd just said. She waited for him to speak. Then, she was afraid he would speak. God, she'd really done it now.

"Hey," he said, and his voice had a smooth, whisper-like ease about it, "you know what?"

She felt vulnerable and sick with embarrassment. "What?"

"I love you, too." He leaned into the window and kissed her. "Now let's go save the world."

8.

Jack knew something was terribly wrong as soon as he saw the driver's side door of Wayne's patrol car standing wide open.

He stopped his own cruiser short and waited for the dust to settle. Nothing moved. With a terrible sinking feeling in his gut he got out, shotgun in hand.

"Hey, Wayne," he yelled.

He waited a beat.

"Wayne?"

No answer. Something was definitely wrong here. He scanned the sage shrubs and mesquite trees that grew along the northern edge of the road, looking for some sign of movement, some indication of what had happened to his deputy, but there was nothing. Nothing but the wind moaning across the desert hardpan.

He went over to Wayne's patrol car and lit up the inside with his flashlight.

No sign of a struggle.

But that didn't mean anything. Just that whatever had gone wrong hadn't gone wrong here, in the car.

"Where did you get on to, Wayne?" Jack muttered.

His gaze drifted up the hill. His daughter and that Cunningham kid had probably been parking up there. It made him sick thinking about it – until he noticed that the top of the hill was lined with a frosty blue light, like moonlight on the grass. But that wasn't right. The moon was in the wrong part of the sky to backlight the hill. It was something else. With his heart beating hard against the walls of his chest, Jack trotted up the hill and looked out over the base.

On the far side of the barracks, about four hundred yards away, a bright blue light was coming from the open front doors of the main hangar. This, he realized, was what Margaret had tried to tell him earlier.

"Ah crap," he said.

But his fatherly remorse soon gave way to his cop instincts. Something was going on down there, and whatever it was, he had a feeling it was something bad.

He should call for cover, he thought. It was the smart thing to do, the safe thing. It's what he would expect one of his deputies to do.

"Screw it," he said, and headed down the hill toward the barracks at a trot.

When he reached the first of the buildings he pressed his back against the wall and tried to blend into the shadows, his senses strained against the darkness. The dilapidated buildings creaked in the desert wind, but he could hear nothing else. No owls; no coyotes in the distance; just the steady whistle of the wind as it seethed through the cracks in the old timber and eddied under the eaves of the barracks.

Jack adjusted his grip on the shotgun.

He glanced around the corner. It looked clear. He took a few deep breaths, then ducked into a crouch and ran for the hangar. He'd almost made it when he saw a sudden flash of movement to his right.

He stopped, threw himself against the nearest wall, and listened.

Something was on the roof above him.

He could hear it tapping against the shingles, coming closer to the edge right over top of him. Jack stood perfectly still, painfully aware of the breath whistling in his nostrils.

Suddenly the tapping stopped, and Jack could feel his blood run cold.

"Please, please –" he whispered.

A thin, sifting stream of dirt fell before his face.

Jack glanced quickly to either side, looking for an escape, and that was when he saw the trail of blood in the dirt. It led to the next building – and to Wayne Givens.

The deputy was cocooned in a gauzy veil of silken spider webs and suspended from an open doorway. Jack could see just enough of the man's face to recognize the wide-eyed horror and pain frozen on his face.

Oh, Wayne, Jack thought. No.

But Jack hadn't even fully absorbed the horror when he saw something moving in the shadows behind the cocoon.

A spider. A giant spider!

Jack's eyes went wide as the spider moved into the moonlight and he realized the full size of the thing. It was – immense – unnatural – its eight eyeballs glistening like pools of motor oil.

The clicking on the roof above him grew frantic, and the next instant something big and gray jumped from the roof and onto the weed-patched lawn between the barracks.

It was another giant spider, every bit as big and hairy and ugly as the first.

The two creatures squared off against one another, their fangs moving up and down in a sort of ritualized sparring match.

141

Moving as quietly as he could, Jack slunk back into the darkness under the eaves of the barracks. The two spiders were still occupied with each other, and that was just fine. It gave him a chance to get the hell out of there.

But he didn't make it far.

No sooner had he stepped out from under the shadows than he stopped, staring in surprise.

A man was coming out of the hangar.

Or was it a man? He didn't look like any man Jack had ever seen around Bristol Plains. And he certainly didn't dress like a local. He wore a shimmering silver costume, skintight, like some kind of crazy flight suit. There was a lightning bolt on the chest, and an imperious, disdainful bearing to him. He held his chin so high.

Then he locked his gaze on his Jack, and for just a fraction of second, the imperious bearing fell away, yielding a look of dismay.

"What are you doing here?" the man said.

"I, uh –" Jack stammered. "I'm the sheriff. Who are you?"

"You Earthmen are a stupid lot. Stupid, stupid, stupid."

"'Earthmen?'" Jack repeated. He had a sudden feeling he was in far deeper waters than he'd guessed.

Before he knew it the man had pulled some kind of crazy ray gun-looking weapon. It all happened so fast, and while Jack was still holding his shotgun, he had clearly lost control of the situation.

Jack put up his hands and started talking, stalling for time. "Wait!" he said. "Just wait, okay? Tell me what this is all about. What is it you want?"

The man smiled. "I am Space Commander Eros, and I am here to save the known Universe from the menace your race represents."

"What?" Jack started to lower his hands. "Us, a threat? We can't even send rockets into space. How can we be a threat to you?"

Eros' eyes narrowed in disdain. "It won't always be so. Your race is on the verge of perfecting atomic science. Our scientists estimate that very soon, your race will develop a doomsday bomb."

"A –doomsday bomb? I –" Jack shrugged his shoulders helplessly. He had no idea what the man was talking about, only that the key to him getting out of this was to make sure Eros kept on talking.

Eros sighed as he continued seemingly content to explain things in great detail. "Gravity and light holds the universe together, Sheriff, down to the subspace level. Your race will one day develop a weapon using solaronite that will cause a gravitational chain-reaction in subspace, and that will cause a cascading explosion of light through all matter in the universe. Life as we know will be destroyed. All life, everywhere."

"But that's not us. We haven't done anything."

"And your objections are not my problem, Earthman."

Behind the man, Jack saw dark flickers in the shadows along the back wall. A moment later, three more of the gigantic spiders emerged and scurried into place on either side of the man.

Jack took a step back - and stopped. There was a noise behind him, a familiar clicking sound. Jack glanced over his shoulder. The first two giant spiders, the ones who had been sparring over Wayne's corpse, were closing in behind him. He was surrounded.

When he looked back toward Eros, the man was still aiming the crazy space gun at him.

Knowing he had only a moment to act, Jack jumped to one side and rolled. And not a moment too soon, Eros had shot some kind of laser ray at him. It missed Jack by inches, charging the air around it and blasting the dirt where he'd just been standing. Jack looked back just long enough to see a blackened, smoking hole in the ground.

He regained his footing and took off running for another large building next to the hangar.

"Get him!" Jack heard Eros shout from somewhere behind him.

Jack looked back and saw two of the spiders jumping from the clearing he'd just abandoned onto the roofs of the nearby barracks. Amazingly, the spiders jumped from one roof to the next with terrifying ease, covering thirty or forty feet with every jump.

One of them managed to get in front of him, landing on the edge of the roof right above Jack. The thing's huge legs flexed menacingly as it stared at him. Its fangs twitched, and as Jack's world tunneled around the tips of those fangs, he actually thought he saw a malignant yellow tear of venom drip to the ground.

"No," he said. "No way."

He jammed his shotgun into the grapelike cluster of eyes above the spider's fangs and fired. The blast flipped the spider over onto its back, where its legs groped uselessly at the sky.

A second spider landed on the roof to Jack's right, then leapt again, this time right at Jack.

Jack shot the creature in mid-air, and it crashed in a heap at his feet.

The other three spiders were quickly closing the distance behind him, bounding from rooftop to rooftop. There was no way he could take them like this, out in the open. He needed to find cover, and fast.

He turned and ran the last fifty feet to the front door of the big building next to the hangar. It was the motor pool, he could see that now, the words painted in faded stenciled letters on the metal door. An imposing padlock secured the chain on the door's handle. Without glancing back he shot the lock away and kicked the door open, running inside and closing it behind him just as one of the spiders slammed into the other side. He looked around frantically for something, anything, he could use to Katy-bar the door.

His eyes fell on a short section of rebar, rusting in the dust. *That'll work*, he thought. He jammed the piece of metal into the brackets on the door and backed away. The spiders hit the door again, causing it to shake against its hinges, but the rebar held. Jack continued to back away. All around him were the rusting hulks of ruined Jeeps and 5-tonners, long forgotten workbenches, and cans of gasoline.

For a moment, he almost let himself believe that he had beaten those spiders. They were outside and he was inside, where he was safe. It wasn't to be, though. The front door was flanked on either side by large panel windows, and Jack noticed them right before the spiders came crashing through in a shower of splinters and flying glass.

Two of them jumped onto the far wall, hanging above the rows of gas cans. The third jumped onto a 5-tonner to Jack's right.

It was close, too close, and moving fast. The thing was less than seven feet from him when Jack managed to squeeze off a shot, blasting away three of its legs and causing it to slide down the front of the truck.

He racked another shell into the breach, put the muzzle against the struggling thing's bizarre, alien face, and fired.

The blast turned the giant spider's abdomen to goo that oozed off and onto the truck's hood and onto the floor.

Jack allowed himself a momentary smile of triumph before making ready again.

One of the two remaining spiders landed on top of the truck, the aging frame creaking and groaning beneath the spider's weight. Jack was about to shoot it when the final spider landed on the truck behind him.

There was only one way to go. He fell to the ground scrambled underneath a truck. One of the spiders jumped after him and squeezed itself under the back bumper. It could barely move its long legs, but it was coming on sure enough. Jack was on his belly and couldn't roll over. But he could see the thing coming and that was enough. He extended the shotgun down past his boots and fired it one-handed at the spider's face.

He didn't stop there, though. He crawled forward, grabbed the truck's front bumper, and pulled himself out into the open -- while turning over as he did.

The other spider was on the hood above him, its fangs poised for the kill.

But Jack was faster. He got his gun up and fired, turning what he could see of the spider to a lumpy, grayish pulp.

With the spider dead, Jack listened to the darkness around him. Was that all of them? He tried to remember. He was pretty sure he'd only seen five, but he wasn't positive.

And he only had one shell left.

Time to lay low, he thought.

He eased back under the truck and waited. Jack listened for a few long moments before he heard it. The distinctive clicking of spider legs on pavement. There was another one in here with him.

He saw it soon after. And this one was immense, bigger than any he'd seen. It was easily the size of the truck under which he was hiding, and as it moved past his position, its legs working in a busy blur of motion, Jack held his breath.

Oh please oh please oh please, he prayed. Dear Jesus, please don't let it see me.

It came up even with his position and hesitated, as though smelling the air, trying to lock onto his scent. Jack had no idea if spiders could smell or not, but that was what it looked like the thing was doing. It was the hunter and he was the prey, and that thing was looking for him.

As it moved, the hairs on its belly twitched and vibrated, as though they too were looking for him, and for a moment, Jack thought he might be ill. He closed his eyes and kept holding his breath.

When he opened his eyes again, the thing was gone.

Jack stared around as much as the truck above him allowed, and that was when he saw the gas tanks on the far wall. Really saw them this time.

And that gave him an idea.

The Allende had burned to the ground. According to the Cunningham boy, the fire had taken all those spiders with it.

That just might work —

9.

Dave and Margaret covered the distance out to Kellman without saying a word. Dave was too intent on his driving; his speed reckless on the old dark roads with nothing but moonlight to guide him. Margaret hated to drive fast - it made her feel helpless - but she didn't say anything to Dave. She was too scared. Earlier, when he came to get her at her bedroom window, all this had felt like a great big adventure, like she was in a romance novel where she was the heroine and Dave was the dangerously handsome highwayman, whisking her away to some scandalous seduction. But as they sped deeper into the night and the craziness of their mission sank in, she grew frightened and withdrawn. Several times she almost told him to stop, turn around, and take her home.

But then they were pulling up onto the ridge that led to the lookout point over the barracks, and it was too late to turn back. Ahead of them, amid a swirling cloud of white dust, they could see two police cars.

"Daddy," Margaret said.

Dave pulled up next to her father's car.

"Not too close, Dave."

"There's nobody here," Dave answered. "See? Look around."

She did, and saw nothing but the empty desert night filling in the spaces around them. It felt large and menacing, as though it might swallow her whole.

"What are we going do?" she asked.

"I don't-"

A sudden gunshot cut him off.

"What was that?"

He didn't even bother to respond. He opened the car door and started trotting toward the hilltop.

"Wait!" she said. "Where are you going?"

"Come on," he said, not even bothering to look back.

Margaret climbed out and went after him. "Dave, wait!"

She stopped at the top of the hill next to him and stared over the barracks. From here, the buildings looked whole, neatly ordered, the product of a utilitarian military mind. But the closer she looked, the more traces of abandonment she could see. Some of the roofs had holes so large they could be seen from here, dark splotches on dusty gray slate.

But nothing moved. There was no trace of the person who had fired the shot. Margaret quickly scanned the whole place: the hangar, the empty barracks, the large, barn like building next to the hangar, the metal communications aerial next to that. Nothing moved.

"There!" Dave said, putting a hand on her shoulder and pointing toward the blue light spilling out of the hangar. "See that?"

She did. A man was there, walking slowly around the hangar's front entrance. He headed toward the door and disappeared into the blue light.

"Who is that?"

"I don't know," he said. "Let's go find out."

"What? No."

But he was already running down the hill. She caught up with him at a busted section of the perimeter fence. He pulled it up with both hands, making a tunnel of a small section of fencing.

"Go on," he said.

"Dave, I'm so scared."

"Me too, Margaret. But it's up to us." Then, more quietly: "Come on. I'm right behind you."

She got down on her hands and knees and crawled through. He

followed her through and they emerged amid the creaking hulks of the abandoned barracks. She looked around, not liking the fetid smell of decay and mold that hung on the breeze. This place had seemed like such a romantic setting when she was in his arms up on the hill earlier in the evening, ready to give herself to him; now, it was claustrophobic, nasty, and unsettling, like a bad place encountered in a dream.

He took her hand and the sudden contact shook her loose from her fear.

"Come on."

Dave pulled her along and she came with him willingly enough. She was frightened, but being with him gave her strength somehow. When they touched, it was enough to make her believe they were something special, invincible, and stronger than either of them by themselves. She liked that about what they had; she loved that. It sustained her, even when they came upon the blasted body of the first giant spider.

"Are you okay?" he asked.

She had bent over and vomited at the sight of the thing. Dave was standing to her side, pulling the hair back from her face.

Margaret nodded.

She wasn't able to speak. The thing was too horrible, too much like a thing from a nightmare.

"Can you walk?"

She nodded again.

He stayed next to her as she stood up.

"Don't look at it," he said. "Come on."

"My Daddy –"

"It's gonna be fine," he said.

She looked at him then, her expression flickering back and forth between anger and the need for reassurance.

"He did this," Dave said. "He's the one who shot this thing." He looked around. "And there. That one over there, too. Your Dad's a trained lawman, Margaret. And a Marine in the Pacific before that. He knows how to take care of himself."

"You're sure he's okay?" She knew he couldn't say for sure, no more than she could, but she needed to hear the words.

"I believe in your Dad," he said. "And I believe in us. Your Dad is here somewhere, but I think he needs help. I think it's up to us."

She stood up straight then, and noticed the look in his eyes.

"Don't kiss me. I'm gross."

He took a handkerchief from his pocket and wiped the corner of her mouth. "You're beautiful, Margaret Summers. You really are. I'd move the world for you."

She was too embarrassed to speak. She took his hand once again and they walked toward the hangar.

But they stopped when they heard voices.

"What's that?" she said.

"Shhh." He crouched down, like he was a cowboy in a serial Western, the Lone Ranger moving into a box canyon.

They stopped at the edge of the hangar door and looked inside. And what they saw took their breath away. The walls were covered with what looked like soap bubbles. The bubbles were hanging like clusters of grapes, each one filled with a writhing shape. On the ground, in front of the bubble cages, were even larger bubbles, beach ball-sized.

Inside, they could see full-grown spiders, some the size of cats, others as big as goats.

They were smaller than the ones they'd seen out among the barracks, but these were active, actually jumping against the walls of the bubbles, causing the whole grapelike cluster to bounce and wobble.

And there was a man standing in the center of the room, a bank of computers formed around him like a horseshoe. In front of him stood some kind of massive television. He was talking to a man's face on the screen, but it took Margaret a second to realize that the man on the TV was talking back to the man.

It wasn't a TV, she realized.

Certainly not a television like any she'd ever seen. It was closer to those vid-screens they had in the science-fiction movies down at the Allende, but unlike the ones down at the Allende, these didn't flicker and dance with bad reception. She'd never seen a picture so clear, so convincingly three-dimensional.

A man in a strange, silvery bodysuit was standing in front of the vidscreen, his back to them.

"This does not negatively impact our operation," the man was saying. "I still have all of my adult specimens and those can be deployed against the Earthlings as planned."

Margaret caught Dave's eye. "'Earthlings?'" she mouthed silently.

He shrugged.

"I am not convinced," said the man on the screen. "In your last progress report, you stated that you would need a contingent of at least forty million spiders to engage and destroy the Earth's combined military forces. From what you tell me, you've lost your entire second generation."

"Yes, but not the breeding stock. That is my point. If I can be allowed another six months, I can have another 200 generations in place. That will more than cover our needs."

"Six months?"

"Yes, Commander Agar. Six months."

"And how will you induce breeding so fast, Eros?"

"I will have to use the local human population as incubation hosts. This is a small town, and fairly isolated from the rest of the country. The same factors that made this a logical location for our base of operations will help us in this regard too. There will be no one to miss these humans."

The man on the screen seemed to consider this. "Very well. I will give you the six months you request, Eros. See to it that you use the time wisely."

The screen went silent, but the man did not move.

Margaret put a hand on Dave's arm. "What did he mean he wanted to use us as incubation hosts?"

"It means we're going to be food for baby spiders."

"Oh my God," she gasped. Only then did she remember the camera. "Dave," she said, "get some pictures of this."

"Oh, right," he said.

Dave raised his camera, focused it, and clicked off a shot. But he hadn't counted on the noise. Neither of them did. Or the flash. They might as well have lit off fireworks for all the noise it made and light it made.

Eros spun around.

"Who are you? Identify yourself."

Dave had managed to get out of the doorway, but it was too late for

Margaret. She was caught standing out in the open. Eros pulled some kind of ray gun and pointed it at her.

"You Earthlings are becoming an annoyance. Now stand still, girl."

He raised his ray gun and took aim. To Margaret, the business end of the ray gun's muzzle looked like the great black eye of a snake. It held her fixed in placed, hypnotized with fear. She could feel her bowels clenching in her gut, and though she tried to speak, tried to beg him not to shoot, the only sound that came from her was a sobbing whimper.

A hand fell on her shoulder and she flinched. The next instant, she was being hurled roughly to one side – right into Dave's arms. And not a moment too soon, for the space where she had just been standing was suddenly filled with a blinding flash, like a lightning bolt.

From inside the hangar, they could hear Eros cursing.

"Dave –" she said.

"No time," he said. "Come on."

He took her by the hand and they started running through the barracks and toward the hill where Dave's Ford waited. Dave was so fast, and she struggled to keep up. Every breath felt like a burning stab in her lungs. Her feet felt like they weighed a ton. And still Dave was running, pulling her, urging her along. "Come on, we can't stop!" He actually seemed to be picking up speed. She tried to tell him to slow down, to wait for her, but couldn't make the words come.

Instead, she fell to one knee.

He stopped, turned, took a step toward her, his hand outstretched.

And then his eyes went wide.

"Oh my God, Margaret. Get up!"

She looked behind her and saw something crazy, something impossible. The spiders they'd seen in Eros' cages were approaching, covering the distance between them in huge bounds. Some scurried on the ground, while others leapt from rooftop to rooftop. A few shot past them and managed to get in front of them.

"Dave!"

"This way," he said, and grabbed her hand and guided her down a long narrow alley between two rows of barracks.

Margaret looked up once and saw some of the bigger spiders leaping over their heads, but unable to squeeze down into the gap between the buildings. The smaller spiders were coming up fast behind them, though not nearly as fast as their larger cousins.

"Where are we going?" she said between heaving breaths.

He didn't answer. There was no time. They were coming up on the end of the alley now, and they were running out of options. He stopped at the edge, just short of the clearing, beyond, which was a large barn like building and the communications aerial. Dave looked from there to the roof, and from the roof to the buildings on either side of them.

"What are you looking for?" she asked.

"Something to use as a weapon."

He reached down into the weeds that had grown up along the base of the building and came up with a long, thin piece of metal.

"Rebar," he said. "There's tons of it. They must have been using this when the base was decommissioned."

He didn't wait for a response. He stepped out into the open and swatted a spider about the size of Jeannie Potts' collie out of thin air. The thing tumbled to the ground at Margaret's feet, made a weak, drunken attempt to get back up and then fell over, where it heaved once and died with a sigh.

"This way," he said. The look in his eyes was frightening – a violence and intensity there she hardly recognized.

She ran to him, letting him lead her without a word.

They stopped at the base of the communications aerial and he gestured her toward the ladder.

"Up?" she said, and craned her neck up the length of the ladder. It was so far up there that the ladder seemed to curve back over itself, so that someone climbing it would actually be suspended over nothing but a sickening emptiness and certain death. She couldn't even see the top.

Just then a spider landed in the clearing behind her.

"Go!" Dave said, holding the piece of rebar out in front of him like a pike. "Go!"

She started to climb, the hem of her skirt blowing madly around her knees in the wind. Margaret looked down in time to see the spider leaping for Dave's chest and Dave jamming the metal spear up into the thing's face. He drove it through the spider's body and flipped it over onto its back, pausing only long enough to wrench it loose.

That was enough for her. She turned her attention back to the rungs just above her and started climbing as fast as her mule-pump shoes would let her.

She didn't dare look down. Dave was right below her, urging her on. *Ridiculously*, she thought of disappointing him letting him down: and because she never wanted do that - would never let herself do that she redoubled her efforts and climbed faster, ignoring the pain in her forearms and in her fingers.

Only when she ran out of ladder did she stop. She emerged onto a rickety metal platform and saw the empty sky all around her; all-too-quickly she became aware of the gray, smoke-like clouds drifting by, and the wind that threatened to pick her up like a mad child with a toy and throw her to the ground. She nearly fainted.

Only Dave's hand on the small of her back, pressing her into the aerial's metal frame, kept her on her feet.

That was when she looked down.

The ground was impossibly far below her. And there were spiders leaping up the ladder, effortlessly clinging to the flimsy metal structure, rocking it back and forth, sending shivers and creaks up its length with every jump.

Dave was standing over the top of the ladder with the rebar in both hands, intent on driving it down into the face of any spider stupid enough to come too close.

Margaret held on tight to the metal frame. She never knew she was afraid of heights, but there was no doubt of it now. The spiders suddenly became a distant threat. The real terror was the limitless emptiness swirling all around her.

She sank down to onto her butt, her fingers locked on the metal girders. She wanted nothing but to close her eyes and forget all of this, forget the wind and the nausea and Dave's enraged screams, but she couldn't. She was a prisoner of her fear, of the distance yawning out beneath her.

Then, Dave was calling her name.

She looked over at him, keeping her eyes open through a sheer act of will, and saw one of the giant spiders land on the metal girders above them, less than a dozen feet away.

Its hideous eyes, all eight of them, rolled toward her at once, wet and black and glistening in the moonlight, and she knew she was the center of its attention.

She screamed, and her screams filled up everything, even the vastness of the empty sky.

10.

Jack was coming around the back corner of the hangar, splashing the last of a ten-gallon gas can on the walls, when he heard the screams. He lowered the gas can with a cold, sickening dread coiling in his gut. Though he'd heard the sound but briefly, he knew that scream. A parent always knows.

"Margaret, no!"

He dropped the gas can and took a few frantic steps toward the hangar, his horror mounting as he realized exactly what was going on.

Beyond the gray roof of the motor pool building, he could see the communications aerial rising against an ashen sky. Near the top of the aerial, hanging on for dear life, were his daughter and the Cunningham boy. Dave was fighting back a dozen or more of the spiders with some kind of improvised club, while the aerial itself seemed to be swaying and creaking as more and more of the spiders jumped toward the crow's nest where the kids were putting up their last stand.

Jack took off running for the corner of the motor pool building. He'd made several trips back and forth from the motor pool to the hangar as he collected the gas cans he'd been using, and during those trips he'd seen a rusting fire escape leading up to the roof. He had no idea if it was still safe to climb or if it would collapse under his weight, but at the moment that was the least of his worries. His daughter's life was on the line, and there was nothing on Earth - or from the stars - that would keep him from fighting for her. He sprinted up the stairs, taking them three at a time.

But then, when he reached the roof, his heart sank.

He had misjudged the distance to the aerial, and badly. The crow's nest was still a good forty feet above him, and the gap between the aerial and the roof, upon which he watched, helplessly, was nearly twice that far.

There was no way the kids could jump that distance. Even Dave Cunningham, as athletic as he was, could never make it.

"Margaret!" he screamed. "Margaret!"

He could see her moving up there, but there was no way to know if she saw him or not. As scared, as she no doubt was, she could very well be slipping into shock.

Dave was putting up a heroic fight, though. Two of the spiders leapt toward him. He swung his metal bar – dimly, Jack realized it must be a piece of the rebar he'd seen lying around everywhere down below – and knocked one of them from the aerial, sending it tumbling down, where it smacked into the ground far below.

The second spider arched high above Dave, its legs flailing, its fangs bristling with menace, only to land on the upturned tip of Dave's spear. Like a grizzled veteran, Dave flipped the spider over onto its back, put his boot against the thing's abdomen, and yanked the spear out.

But for all Dave's bravery, there were just too many of them.

Jack's gaze moved down the length of the ladder. It was covered with a writhing carpet of spiders, thousands of them. They were a blur of movement, like static on the TV. Jack was helpless to do anything about it; all he could do was stand there, shaking his head in impotent disbelief, as his daughter screamed away her final seconds.

A sudden jolt shook the aerial.

He looked down to the base and his mouth open in horror.

There was the giant spider that had stalked him earlier in the motor pool, and that he had only barely managed to escape. Now it was lunging up the aerial, its weight and the force of the impact whenever it landed causing the crow's nest to rock back and forth violently.

Several spiders slipped from the metal girders and fell to their death.

Dave lost his footing and landed next to Margaret, who was screaming over and over, every terrible peal wrenching another piece of Jack's heart from his chest.

He watched the thing gaining distance up the aerial, his mind rebelling against the size of it. The spider was easily as big as a milk truck, and as it climbed higher, the force of its landings moved the aerial in an ever-increasing sway. Even from where he stood, Jack could hear the metal groaning and creaking, and faintly, from somewhere under the moving carpet of spiders, the sounds of rusted nuts and bolts snapping.

It's going to fall, he thought. *My God, it really is.*

"Margaret!"

But it was too late. The giant spider was less than twenty feet from the crow's nest, its weight rocking the aerial back and forth like the bob of an enormous, inverted pendulum. The smaller spiders were falling off by the dozens now, dropping to their deaths in a silent shower.

It didn't slow the giant spider, though. It kept coming, relentless, remorseless, a silent hunter intent on its prey.

And then all at once, in an explosion of snapping metal against a prolonged groaning sigh, the aerial gave way and slowly began to lean down toward the very spot where Jack stood.

He could barely believe his eyes. His daughter was there, blind with tears, a death grip on the metal girders, with the Cunningham boy right beside her. She was less than seven feet away now, a distance she could make.

"Margaret!" he screamed. "Margaret, look at me!"

She was trembling, but his voice got through her fear somehow. Margaret turned toward him, but without a trace of recognition in her wild, mad stare.

"Jump to me!" he said, his hand outstretched.

The spider was less than a dozen feet from them now. It had lost its hold on the girders when the aerial collapsed, but it was still hanging on by two of its spindly legs.

Jack refused to look at it. He focused everything he had on Margaret, willing her to meet his gaze.

"Margaret!"

She was trying, but the fear was too great, and she could only manage to shake her head and move her mouth in a vague pantomime of screams.

He turned to the Cunningham boy. Dave too had managed to hang on - literally. He was hanging from a crossbeam like a man struggling to do one more pull up.

"Dave," Jack said. "Get up. Get up!"

Every muscle in Dave's body was tensed to the breaking point. The veins in his neck were standing out like cords, his arms trembling.

"For God's sake, Dave. She needs you. Please!"

Watching the boy struggle was maddening. He wanted so badly to will his strength to the boy, to force him, cajole him, reach down and pull him up by his hair if necessary – but none of that was possible. All Jack could do was beg Dave to find the strength inside himself to gain the girder from which he was hanging.

"Please," he muttered. "Please, Dave."

Inch by painful inch, the boy somehow managed to pull himself up. First, he got an elbow over the top edge of the girder, then, by rocking himself back and forth, got a knee hooked over the same girder. Dave rested for just a moment, his chest heaving, then pulled himself up the rest of the way.

"Help her!" Jack shouted.

But Dave was already doing that. He knelt down at Margaret's side and held her face in his hands. At first she continued to shake, her eyes unseeing, but then something happened. Jack, no stranger to body language, saw a sea change in his daughter. Where his yelling had failed to reach her, Dave's hands cradling her cheeks had calmed her. She was staring into his eyes now, and calm, like she had found her center.

Her hands came loose from the girder and wrapped around Dave's neck.

The boy then pulled her to her feet, and led her over to the edge of the sideways crow's nest. She was standing on a swaying strip of metal now, nothing to hold on to but Dave's hand.

"You can do it, Margaret," Jack said. "Come on, jump. I'll catch you."

"I can't," she groaned.

"You can. Come on now, Margaret. Jump!"

She looked back at Dave, who nodded. Then the boy put his hands on Margaret's waist and added his heave behind her jump. For a painfully long moment she was suspended in space, eighty feet above the ground, before landing in Jack's outstretched arms. He caught her and the two of them fell back onto the slate roof.

Jack held her close, and for a moment that seemed suspended in eternity, he thought the body he held was that of the two-year-old toddler who would always come giggling to meet him at the door when he came home from a long shift on patrol. Only when she pulled herself to her feet and said, "Dave," did the feeling of warmth and comfort that had swelled up within him fade away.

When he climbed to his feet his daughter was standing on the edge of the roof, yelling for her boyfriend to jump.

Dave took a long look down. The giant spider was still there. It was pulling its legs together, grouping them on the girder from which it hung. And then, with terrible sureness, it pulled itself close to the metal and flipped over onto the top of the girder. It was on its feet now, ready to pounce.

Jack added his voice to Margaret's. He yelled for Dave to jump.

Dave took a step back, and when he did, the metal structure beneath him dropped again. It crumpled over, the light box that had once crowned the crow's nest now an arm's length below the level of the roof. Yet Dave retained his footing. He was crouched down now, looking up at Jack and Margaret, the giant spider climbing up toward him.

"Jump!" Jack yelled. "Now!"

The next instant, Dave was sailing through the air. He jumped up toward Jack's outstretched hand and caught it, but only by the fingertips.

Jack fell forward, straining with all he had to hold onto the boy.

Jack had barely enough time to look across the gulf to where the spider was beginning its leap that would land it on the roof. He gave one last mighty heave and pulled Dave up and onto the roof.

At the same time, the spider jumped at them.

But the force of its takeoff must have shifted the balance of metal and gravity-to-gravity's favor, for it had yet to launch itself completely when the entire communications aerial collapsed in a shriek of metal and dying spiders. As Jack focused his gaze beyond the terrified face of the Cunningham boy, he saw spiders and aerial alike crumpling toward the ground far below in a roar of groaning metal.

And so too was the giant spider. It tumbled end over end toward the ground, and when it hit, Jack could hear the satisfying thud of its enormous body smacking into the hard packed desert soil far below.

A moment later he was pulling Dave onto the roof.

The three of them sat there for a few stunned seconds, unable to completely digest what had happened, and then Margaret started to laugh.

The sound caught Jack by surprise.

He looked to his daughter, but she wasn't looking back at him. She was looking at Dave Cunningham.

And Dave was looking back at her, a huge grin on his face.

Surprisingly, Jack felt no resentment, no hurt. This was, he knew, the way it was supposed to be. She had found the man she was meant to be with, and rather than feel as though he had lost her, he knew on some deeper level that he had succeeded. Everything in his life had been directed toward giving her this moment, and even if they had been at the end of an aisle in the middle of a great big church, with him about to give his daughter away in marriage, the moment could not have felt more real, more complete.

11.

But the moment did not last. Hundreds of spiders had already fallen from the toppled communications aerial, hopefully to their death, but a great many more were still climbing, inching closer to the crow's nest.

"We have to go," Dave said.

Margaret brushed the hair out of her eyes and grabbed Jack's hand. "Daddy, we heard that spaceman down there. He wants to use us as spider food."

Before Jack could speak, Dave jumped to her defense.

"She's right, Sheriff. We heard him talking on that TV in his lab. He wants to use the people of Bristol Plains as food for those giant spiders. We heard him say he needed six more months before he had enough of those spiders to take on the military. We have to stop him. We tried to get pictures, but I dropped the camera."

"His name is Eros," Jack said.

"What?" Dave said. He looked at Margaret.

"Daddy?" she said.

"I had a run in with him, too," Jack explained. "He told me his name was Eros. He didn't tell me about the spiders, but he told me he was here to kill us."

"But why?" asked Margaret.

"Apparently, sometime in the future, we're going to build some kind of forbidden weapon. He called it a 'doomsday bomb.' He said it would cause some kind of cascading nuclear reaction throughout the known universe. It would destroy everything on the atomic level, apparently."

Margaret put a hand over her mouth. "Oh my God."

"Yeah," Jack said.

"So what do we do?" Dave asked. "I don't know about you, but I'm not gonna let him kill us all just because of something we may or may not do in the future."

"I agree," Jack said. He was really beginning to like this boy. "I've got a plan. But first we need to get off this roof and back to my patrol car up above the barracks." He looked over the edge of the roof, down at the swarm of spiders clustered around the communications aerial. "No idea how we're gonna do that, though."

"I think I have an idea," Dave said.

Jack raised an eyebrow.

To Margaret, Dave said, "Remember that alleyway between the buildings we took to get here?"

"Yeah," she said, her eyes suddenly bright with hope. "Daddy, it goes all the way across the base. It's real narrow. The big ones can't get down into it, and the smaller ones get all bunched up when they try to follow you through it. It slows them down."

"That's right," Dave agreed. "We could take it about midway across the barracks area and then cut back toward our cars."

"You're talking about a flanking maneuver," Jack said.

"Yeah," he said, and stopped himself. "I mean, yes sir."

Jack smiled, and then nodded. "Okay," he said. "Let's get moving."

12.

Jack had figured the hardest part would be crossing the open patch of ground between the corner of the motor pool and the entrance to the alleyway, but they made it with little trouble, and, as far as he could tell, without being seen.

They weren't followed through the alleyway, nor did they see any signs of danger as they worked their way across the base and up the hill to where his car was parked. He was beginning to think they'd got off easy, but as it turned out, the hardest part came when they reached the car.

"I'm not staying here," Margaret said.

She had her arms crossed over her chest, her foot planted firmly in the dirt where she had just stamped it.

"I didn't tell you to stay here," Jack responded. "I told the two of you to head back into town and get the rest of my deputies out here. Now move."

Neither kid gave an inch.

"Margaret," Jack said, his patience all but gone, "I'm not playing with you. I told you to do something and I expect you to do it. Don't make me tell you again."

"I'm coming with you, Daddy."

He almost slapped her. He was ready to pick her up fireman carry style and throw her into the backseat, maybe the boy too, when Dave said, "I need to come with you."

That stopped Jack in his tracks.

"What did you say?"

"You're gonna need help," Dave said. "There's no way you can drive and light the flares at the same time. Not with those spiders all over the place."

Jack opened his mouth to object, but then stopped. As much as he hated to admit it, the boy was right. He would need both hands to drive. Setting the gas he'd put down on fire would require a second person to light and throw the road flares. He could go back to town and get his deputies himself, but that dog wouldn't hunt and he knew it. By the time they organized and came back here, Eros would have had time to regroup and prepare for their arrival - or worse, take his show on the road to some other town that didn't have the faintest idea of what was going on. So, he couldn't go alone, and he couldn't leave the fight to someone else. He was going to have to bring the boy.

And that left Margaret. He couldn't very well leave her here, and she couldn't drive herself. He'd been too old-fashioned to give his permission for his little girl to learn to drive because women didn't drive, not in Texas anyway. At least, that's what he'd always told himself. But now, considering the situation that way of thinking created, he felt ridiculous.

Well, he thought, *as soon as we get out of this, she learns to drive.*

He turned to Dave.

"You know how to work those flares?"

Dave nodded, his expression grave. "I do."

"Margaret," Jack said, "you're up front with me."

Less than a minute later they were speeding down the hillside, headed toward a collision with the chain link fence around the base.

"Hold on," Jack said, putting an arm across Margaret, much as he'd done when she was a child riding next to him and he'd had to stop suddenly.

Jack mashed down on the gas, and the car hurtled through the fence, never slowing down, even as they hit loose gravel and began to fishtail.

"Daddy!"

"I got it," he said irritably, and wrestled the steering wheel back under control while simultaneously easing off the gas. Once he had them going straight again, he put the gas pedal to the floor and charged.

They had gone maybe halfway to the main hangar when they saw the first of the spiders. The creatures were jumping from the rooftops down onto the car, striking its sides and roof with dull, hard thuds. Then one of the larger ones jumped directly into their path. Jack turned just in time and the thing smashed into the grill near the right side headlight before falling under the vehicle and into the track of the front tire. The impact sent a shudder through the car, and when the car bounced over the dead spider the feeling reminded Jack of running over a set of railroad tracks while going too fast.

But he had come this far and had no intention of slowing down, no matter what horrors got in his way. He kept both hands gripped tightly on the wheel and his foot firmly planted on the floorboard.

"Uh, Sheriff–" Dave said.

"I see him."

Ahead, through the swarm of spiders and clouds of dust, silhouetted by the blue light from the lab, was Eros. He was walking out of the hangar, his ray gun in his hand, a look of utter contempt and mounting rage darkening his features.

"He's gonna shoot at us," Margaret said.

"I see it."

The first blast from Eros' ray gun streaked past Jack's side of the car, missing them by inches.

"Shit," he growled, giving the wheel a hard jog to the right.

Eros was firing rapidly now, but Jack kept the car moving, veering hard from one side of the narrow lane to the other in a constant serpentine track. They were closing on the hangar at well over sixty miles an hour, dodging a constant barrage of laser beams from Eros, and still Jack kept the petal to the floor.

"Be ready with that flare," he said to Dave.

Dave nodded. He pulled up a handful of road flares from the floorboard and struck one. Instantly, the inside of the car began to glow with a pinkish red light from the hissing flare.

"On my mark," Jack said.

"Ready," answered Dave.

Jack pointed the car to the right, then brought it back hard to the left and immediately back to the right again, sending the car into a drift intended to carry them alongside the enormous hangar while simultaneously kicking up a rooster-tail of dust to cover their tracks.

The last Jack saw of Eros was the wide-eyed look of surprise and fear in the spaceman's stare as they shot past him.

The next instant, Eros was enveloped by the cloud of dust and they were speeding along the outside wall of the hangar. Jack pointed the car away from the building slightly and gave the order for Dave to throw the first flare.

Dave leaned out the passenger side window and arched it over the roof of the car. Looking into his rearview mirror, Jack saw the first flames starting to catch.

"Excellent," he said. "Again."

They sped around the back of the building; Jack slowed down just enough to allow Dave to throw the last of the flares. The kid was still leaning out the window when a huge spider jumped onto the roof.

"Dave!" Margaret reached over, grabbed Dave by the belt, and pulled him back inside the car.

The look on his face was one of pure fear.

"That was close," he managed to say.

"Get your window up!" Jack yelled. He was already rolling his up. The spiders were falling on the car from every direction now, hitting the hood, the roof, the doors, busting the windshield. As they careened around the front of the building, the giant beasts were so thick on the windshield that Jack could no longer see. He was driving blind, hoping that they weren't headed straight into a ditch or the side of a building, when all at once they ran over something and the car went into a yaw. It spun in nearly a full circle, coming to a stop with the engine stalled.

Jack tried to restart the engine, but all it would do was cough. Meanwhile the spiders were dropping onto the car in greater and greater numbers. They were so thick Jack could only see fleeting glimpses of what was happening outside. But that was enough. They had stopped less than a car's length from the building. The fires they had started were beginning to catch. Flames were climbing the sides of the hangar, fingers of fire reaching up to the roof in some parts.

And through the smoke and flames and massing spiders, Jack thought he saw Eros turning in disgust from the scene and heading back into the hangar.

But what for?

The question was answered by a roar a moment later. The sound shook the ground and the car, and it got louder with every passing second, until finally it felt to Jack like he was standing next to a huge train as it sped past.

"Daddy, what is that?" Margaret yelled.

Jack couldn't answer. In the military he'd learned to keep his mouth open and his hands clapped over his ears to equalize the pressure of exploding shells, and he was doing that now.

But he still wasn't expecting the blast when it came.

Suddenly the night grew intensely bright as a white fireball rolled out of the hangar and washed over the police car.

When it subsided, several seconds later, the few spiders that remained on the outside of the car were burnt and smoking, all of them dead. The roar too was subsiding, and it left Jack stunned, unable to fully understand what had just happened. The hangar, he could see now, was a blasted ruin, and an orange wall of fire was climbing high up into the desert sky.

"Look!" Dave said, pointing at the sky through the blackened, soot-stained windshield.

Still in a stunned stupor, Jack followed the track of the Cunningham boy's finger. The explosion had blasted the roof off the hangar, and rising up through that gaping hole, Eros' spaceship was mounting to the stars, racing away at incredible speeds.

All Jack could do was watch and shake his head. Even now, as he was watching it happen, he could barely believe it.

He looked down at his daughter. Her face was caked with dirt and grime, but otherwise she was none the worse for wear. Seeing her, he was suddenly overcome with a crazy, wonderful sense of joy.

And he began to laugh.

13.

High above the Earth, Eros was in a foul temper.

He stared out the view port watching his labors burn to the ground. It was still inconceivable to him the humans had managed to undo everything he'd worked for - again! But there it was, burning.

It was maddening. How had it happened? Looking over his Plan, he couldn't find a single mistake or missed step. The humans possessed no major weapons, no special strengths or other talents. They had only their courage, their drive, and their fighting spirit; in this case, like every other Plan throughout their history, that had been enough. If he hadn't exactly believed the predictions made by the scientists in the Alien Technology Forecasting Division that one day these people would invent the dreaded doomsday bomb, the events of this night had convinced him. This was not a race to be trifled with.

But neither was he.

Eros drummed his fingers on his chair and thought through the details of his next Plan. The Plan that would convince not only The Ruler but also

165

the High Council that he finally had the humans where he wanted them. Next time, he would need to come prepared for a real battle.

But first, of course, he'd need to convince Agar.

Eros glanced at the Televisor and frowned. He wasn't looking forward to that conversation.

But Agar could wait for a few moments. He reached into the storage compartment next to his chair and produced the only one of the specimen cages he'd managed to salvage from lab so he could see inside. A tiny scytode lay dead inside.

Eros sighed as his mind spun. Suddenly, he bolted out of his chair, crossing the span of the bridge in a few quick running steps. In front of a workspace at the side of the room, he put the small cage down on the table and grabbed his newest invention. He held the strange-looking gun up to his face, and his smile grew wide.

Pointing the apparatus at the cage, he activated the Electrode Ray. It's coils hummed with otherworldly energy as its beam enveloped the scytode inside.

After a moment, he set the Electrode Ray down and tapped the plate near the spider. After the briefest of moments, it twitched and spasmed, finally standing upright on its eight legs. Where Eros had expected it to be agitated and active, the creature stood stoic with its eyes fixated on him, as if awaiting further instructions.

Eros' smile turned into a fiendish grin.

Yes, Agar could wait.

For now, it was time to sit and work out the details of Plan 9.

I owe a huge thanks to Ray Bradbury for this story. I am not going to say why. It is a secret I told Mr. Bradbury I'd take to the grave. And Donn Albright deserves a huge thanks too. This is one of the few stories in the book that you can read to your children or grandchildren at night and it won't give them nightmare. Nevertheless, I hope you enjoy this tale about trolls...

THE STONE BRIDGE TROLLS
by Michael McCarty

It was a very special bridge made of old stones and always shadowy underneath, especially on the sunniest, hottest days. It smelled of watery film, shells, crayfish, and wet mud under there. And the two girls, thumping across the bridge, hand in hand, their hair like similar blonde flags streaming behind them, paused to smell, sniff, and shout at the slowly flowing water.

"This is a bridge," said Nancy, "and trolls live under bridges."

"You've heard of trolls?" asked Ellen.

Nancy nodded slowly. "Sure. Who hasn't?"

"My father says there's a troll under every bridge and if you stray or are bad or throw rocks, the trolls'll get you."

"Bosh!" said Nancy, remembering to imitate her Grandmother.

"No, really."

"Trolls and elves and Santa Claus—ha!"

"Don't laugh, the trolls'll hear you!"

"Ha ha, trolls!"

"I've always wanted to be a troll. Wouldn't it be fun, hiding under here, nobody knowing, all the time peeking out, snatching bad children and eating them?"

"Bones and all?"

"Of course! It would be fun, wouldn't it?"

"Yeah, I guess it would!"

"Let's play trolls!"

And so they played.

Two trolls sat suspended on the crossbeams under the bridge. They

167

watched the fair-haired girls through the wooden planks with wide-eyed fascination. The first troll was a gnarly gray furry creature with sharp fangs. The other troll was covered in bushy black brush. He had twitching pointed ears and a wicked smile.

The girls used the bridge as a stage to do their grand performance as trolls. Nancy swayed her arms back and forth as she walked, then growled. Ellen leaned over the rails and held her mouth wide apart with her fingers.

Neither of the girls spotted the spying trolls below.

"This is an insult!" said the gray troll, growling with irritation.

"Huh?"

"Those foolish girls are trying to act like trolls."

"So?"

"That isn't how we act."

"They're just little girls."

"It isn't even a close imitation of a troll. I don't need fingers to hold my mouth that wide open. They aren't even flicking their tongues or hanging upside down with their toes."

The black troll sighed.

"It isn't even scary. We can be scary!"

"Of course."

"We could do a better imitation of little boys than they can of trolls."

The black troll thought about it for a moment. He scratched his furry head and suddenly his wicked grin widened. "We'll see about that." And with a snap of his clawed fingers, the trolls instantly became handsome little boys.

Nancy and Ellen couldn't help but notice the two good-looking boys on the other side of the bridge. They even started to cross the bridge, coming their way.

"We're trolls," said Nancy.

"Yeah, trolls! So watch out!" said Ellen.

"You look like little girls to us," said the boy who used to be a black troll.

Silence ensued. It didn't matter that the lads didn't talk much because Nancy and Ellen were smitten by them. The girls quickly ran off the bridge, giggling every step of the way. When the boys made it across, the girls picked some flowers and returned to them.

"I'm Nancy."

"I'm Ellen."

The boys stood smiling.

"What are your names?" asked Nancy.

"I'm Hollis."

"I'm Stone."

The girls gave the boys the freshly picked flowers. Hollis and Stone looked at the black-eyed Susans, bleeding hearts, and impatiens with confusion.

"Silly boys," said Nancy. "You sniff flowers."

Hollis put the flowers to his nose and sniffed. They did smell nice — nice enough to eat. He chewed on them and Stone joined in, feasting on the bouquets.

"If you two are that hungry," said Ellen, "maybe you should join us in a picnic."

The food was plentiful and delicious. Liverwurst sandwiches with speared dill pickles and hot mustard on dark pumpernickel bread, potato chips, cupcakes — and to wash it all down, bottles of cold root beer.

Stone let out a loud burp after he was finished eating. He quickly covered his mouth. *No human boy would belch after a meal.* He thought, *I've blown my cover! They know my true troll identity now.*

"Boys can be so gross," said Nancy.

"Yeah, gross," Ellen said, staring dreamily at Hollis.

Stone was staring dreamily, too — at the herd of goats across the field. Although he had just finished a good meal, what troll could resist a goat snack?

"What are you looking at?" asked Nancy, curious of the lad's obsessive gaze at the billy, nanny, and kids in the meadow.

Stone didn't answer the girl's question. Instead he jumped over the wooden fence and ran after the herd. In a few seconds, he was gone from sight.

"Boys can be so weird, too" said Nancy.

Before Nancy could get in another good barb about the nature of boys, her mother called her home.

Hollis and Ellen watched Nancy run home.

"I suppose I should be leaving, too," said Ellen. "Before I leave, please give me a kiss. I want to see if you are my Prince Charming or just a frog."

"A kiss?" he replied. "No! That would—"

Before he could finish the sentence, Ellen's lips touched his. At that moment, the spell vanished and Hollis returned to his natural troll state— gray shaggy fur, sharp claws, and fangs for teeth.

The kiss turned Ellen into a cute blonde troll.

"You were a troll, too?" asked Hollis, confused.

"I've always wanted to be a troll. Maybe when I kissed you, my wish came true. Kind of like kissing a frog to turn it into a prince, but in reverse. Sort of."

"Yeah. Sort of." Hollis bared his fangs in a big smile.

The two trolls strolled hand in hand into the shadows under the bridge. Where they lived happily ever after.

Connie Sherwood was the editor of the ezine Dark Krypt, which I also wrote for. We talked for years of doing a short story together. It was great, that we finally were able to.

I started reading Stephen King novels in junior high school. The first novel I read was CARRIE. My mom didn't want me to read the book because I was too young, but I got up in the middle of the night to read it. I've been hooked ever since. Stephen King is the reason I'm writing horror in the first place. This story was inspired by the Master of Modern Horror. Connie and I hope you enjoy this twisted tale.

THE COLLECTIVE
by C. L. Sherwood and Michael McCarty

Penny and Nicole Wise shared nothing more in common than being fifteen-year-old identical twins. Penny sat cross-legged on the bedroom floor near an array of clown dolls, stuffed likenesses, and plastic blowups surrounding her. Clowns adorned every inch of her small boxy room from puzzles, posters, bobble-heads, and figurines, to caricatures, drawings, paintings, sculptures, and busts.

"Don't worry," Penny said, "you're not scary to me."

"What about Nicole?" a scratchy, all too familiar snake-like voice asked.

"Nicole will come around," Penny said.

Nicole stood in the hall. "Who are you talking to?"

"No one."

"Well, I'm going to order pizza. You interested?"

"Of course." Penny looked up pushing her too long bleached-blonde bangs off her face. "Come in," she beckoned with an index finger. "We'll order pizza together."

Nicole shifted from foot to foot. "Um – no thanks." She dialed the number on her cell and went back into her bedroom and shut the door. Unlike the calliope of color in her sister's room, these four walls were immaculately white no posters donned them. The room was bare – only a twin-sized bed, desk, computer and a few fantasy books were found.

Thirty minutes later, Nicole returned to Penny's room. "The pizza's here."

"Bring it in here, we can share it. Together, forever."

"No way."

Penny shook her head and laughed. "You're such a wuss." She picked up a stuffed clown and tossed it at Nicole.

Nicole jumped back and tripped, landing squarely on her backside. "That is not a bit funny, Penny! I'll be downstairs. If you want pizza, you'll come down and get some." She picked herself up.

Penny's phone chirped.

Are you girls doing okay? Did you get the money I left on the counter?

Penny rolled her eyes.

We're fine. Eating pizza. See u 2nite.

She set the phone aside. Her mom acted so caring, but she was never around. Even when she was around, she was still absent, unless, of course, one of them did something they shouldn't. She was always around for that. Other than the rare visitor, their single mother, Miranda, cared little about their teen activities or conflicts. She worked two jobs that had her rise early and arrive home late. She was a good mother in some respects, Penny thought. She provided for them – food was always in the fridge, allowances left on the table, and a list of chores on the counter – even if they lacked a close bond. She supposed she understood her mother's behavior, well, at least some of it anyway. Without warning, good ol' dad had departed this world when she and Nicole were just nine years old. Since then, her mother's time was split between "must haves" and "have tos," and there was little room for anything else. She and Nicole filled the void of their mother's absence with online friends, games, and hobbies.

"Pizza's getting cold!" Nicole's high-pitched voice rang out. "If you don't come down, I'll eat it all."

"Be right down!"

Penny rose on her tingling pins-and-needles legs. "I'll be back in a few," she said to the array of clowns. A chill swept over her bare neck and down her back, and she felt a kiss of ice against her check.

Bring Nicole, the scratchy voice said.

"I will. I know she'll just love you once she gets to know you."

Nicole sat on the couch, remote in one hand and a slice of pizza in the other. Penny plopped down beside her. "I'll eat pizza with you, Nicole, but I'm not watching reality TV." She snatched the remote from her sister, flicked through the television menu and snagged a slice of pizza. She wasn't normally a nervous person, but she had to find a way to get Nicole to her bedroom. "Do you want to catch a movie tonight or maybe go to the mall and hang out at the game center?"

Nicole cringed and her shoulders sank. "I hate going to the movies with you. You always want to watch something scary. I think I'd prefer the mall trip, but I want to shop, maybe at Nordstrom's."

"You're joking, right?" Penny said around a mouth full of pizza. "Why would you waste your money in Nordstrom's when you can just go to Hot Topic. The clothes are epic in there."

Nicole eyed Penny with disdain, "*Because* I don't wear Anime or rocker t-shirts or *The Death Squad*. That's why."

"It's *The Suicide Squad*. Harley Quinn and The Joker are awesome!"

"*Death Squad, Suicide Squad*. Whatever. I'd rather go without clothes than wear those," she said dismissively.

"Really?" Penny said. "Well I do. How about we go together and come home together, but don't, you know, actually hang out?"

"Fine by me," Nicole said, dabbing her mouth with a napkin. She started to get up.

"But first," Penny began chewing the pizza, "you need to come up to my room. I'll show you how to dress so guys actually look at you."

Nicole froze. She looked at Penny. "Never," she said firmly and sat again. "I'm not going in that clown-infested dungeon of yours. Ever." She grabbed another slice of pizza, bit and tugged at the cheese, shaking her head like a dog with a rope.

"What is it with you and clowns anyway? We never talk about that," Penny said.

Nicole kept eating the pizza, pretending to be interested in the show on the television.

"They're just clowns, you know. Funny. Besides, I'm only asking you to look at some of my clothes so maybe you can look cool for the trip to the mall," Penny said.

Nicole gave her a killer glance.

"Fine," Penny said, "Just don't look at the clowns. Focus on the clothes."

As the silence lengthened, Penny wondered if she'd gotten Nicole to think about coming up to her room. "We'll have fun trying on stuff. Isn't that what girls like you enjoy? Besides, we never do anything together."

"Untrue," Nicole said, ignoring the shot about being girly. "We're doing something together right now. We're eating pizza, while you try to get me in that clown dungeon of yours. Funny? Not. Creepy? Yes." She shot Penny a hate-filled glance. "Nothing you've asked before has worked and this isn't going to, either. I will not go into that room, no matter what you offer me, even if you offered to toss that IT bust out onto the driveway and burn every Stephen King movie and book you own!"

Penny checked her anger. "I happen to love Stephen King, something I know you don't understand. Besides, I would never offer any of that and you know it." Penny squeezed her pizza slice so tightly the crust ripped. "So nothing else, huh?"

"Nothing."

Her tastes were so different, but – Nicole liked girly things and she loved to shop. Ugh. Penny preferred online shopping. "How about my share of our allowances for the next three weeks?"

"Nope."

"Okay, then. How about my share of our allowances for three weeks and I do your chores for a week?"

"Nope."

Penny punched Nicole in the arm. "Jesus! What will it take to go into my room for, say, fifteen minutes?"

Nicole seemed to think about this idea. She chewed slow and steady, staring ahead. She dabbed at her mouth with a napkin. "Nothing is worth fifteen minutes. But, I will take your offer to step into and out of the room."

Penny laughed and had to shove the pizza back into her mouth. "In and out? That's it? No way."

That's all we need, Penny. Bring her, the scratchy snake-like voice whispered close to Penny's ear. *She'll like us after that.*

Penny almost dropped the slice of pizza in her hand, eyes widening.

She'd never heard the clowns outside her room before. She had no fear of the clowns or the voice, but this felt – different. She'd been trying to get Nicole back into her room since their mother split them up over five years ago. Nicole had nightmares about the clowns and the two fought all the time. "Okay. I will," she whispered.

"You will what?" Nicole asked.

Penny cleared her throat. "I'll make the deal for a couple of seconds in my room."

Nicole grinned. "I guess you won't be going to the mall with me after all."

"Funny," Penny said, stuffing the last of her pizza into her mouth. She wiped her hands. "Let's do it."

Nicole followed Penny upstairs, but stopped short of entering.

Penny opened her closet door wide and made a grand gesture, bowing. "See?"

Nicole shifted and twisted her hands, her eyes darting in all directions. "I don't know," she said.

Pull out the pink skirt and black lace top. She'll like that, the snake voice whispered.

"Awe, come on," Penny said. "It's just in and out." She took a few steps toward Nicole. "You never know. You might end up liking something." Penny turned back to the closet and pulled out a lacy pink short skirt with a matching black lacy top. "Look. I bet you'd look killer in this outfit."

Nicole studied the outfit. Her eyes sparkled.

Penny knew she had her. "You could wear pink lacy tights and your black high heels with it, even carry a cute bag!"

"They are not 'high heels,'" Nicole corrected. "They are stilettos." Nicole placed one foot over the threshold. "It is cute."

Penny jiggled the outfit on the hanger. "I know, right?! Come on. Try it."

Yesssss. The snake voice hissed.

Penny felt suddenly uncomfortable. She rushed forward and met her sister just inside the door. "Here, go try it on so I can see."

Noooo! the voice hissed. *She must come inside!*

Nicole grabbed the hanger and was gone.

"What is going on with you guys?" Penny asked.

The IT bust sitting on her bookshelf glowed and the face animated. *We are hungry. We are lonely.*

"But you have me," Penny said. "We do everything together. What do you need her for?"

Off to her left a stuffed clown in her reading chair stood and pointed. *Because we are hungry. Take care of us and we'll take care of you.*

"You keep saying you're hungry. You don't eat food."

Silly girl! Not your food!

Penny spun.

A clown doll crawled from her bed, fell to the floor, and teetered to her. *Soul. We are hungry. Bring Nicole.*

Fear pricked the hairs on the back of Penny's neck for the first time since she'd started hearing the voices and the clowns had begun moving. "If you're so hungry, what have you been eating all these years?"

The doll fell still on the floor. On her dresser a bobble head began to shake in a jerking motion. *You have little soul left. To continue to eat will bring death. Bring Nicole and live — or die and join us forever.* The head stilled.

"You know," Nicole said standing at the door. "I think I really do like this!"

Penny rushed to the door and pushed Nicole back into the hall. "Good, you can have it. I'll get ready and we'll go, okay?"

"What the crap, Penny?" She straightened herself out. "Did you decide that losing your allowance is a problem?"

Penny felt icy fingers on her shoulders. "Yeah, I decided I'd rather go shopping. Finish getting ready. I'll meet you downstairs."

Nicole shrugged. "Okay."

Penny took a deep breath. "Are you going to hurt her?"

The bust animated. *Are you hurt? Are you in pain? Just eat.*

She could let them feed. The thought made her stomach lurch. The act would buy her some time to decide what to do.

"Are you coming or what?" Nicole yelled.

"Come up. I have something to go with your outfit," she yelled.

Nicole appeared in the doorway. "What is it?"

Penny dug through a drawer, her heart pounding. She produced a little red and black lace bag. "This," she said, holding the bag up.

"Oh, that's cute," Nicole said.

"Come get it. It'll seal our deal."

Nicole's trotted in a bit like a ballerina in her heels and grabbed the bag. As she trotted back toward the door, it slammed.

"What are you doing?" Penny yelled at the clowns.

Eat, came the snake voice. *Eat now.*

Penny ran to the door and tugged. The knob was ice cold and it wouldn't budge.

Nicole's eyes widened. "What's happening?" she screamed.

Penny wrapped her arms around her sister. "Leave her alone!"

"What are you doing?" Nicole said, "Let me go!"

Penny squeezed tighter. "I'm trying to save you," she whispered.

Eat? Yes, eat.

"Don't you eat my sister!" Penny screamed.

Not us. You.

Bells clanged inside Penny's head and she released Nicole, who crumpled to the floor. Penny gazed down – Nicole's shriveled body, eyes sunken, mouth still wide open in her last scream. "You ate her! You hurt her! You promised!" She ran to the window and began chucking her clown collection to the pavement below. After the first three pieces, she hesitated, a glass figurine in her hands above her head. Lowering it, she pulled it close to her heart. "I'm so s-s-sorry. I didn't mean — "

Come to us.

Penny ran downstairs, into the dusky twilight, and knelt near the broken, mangled clown pieces. They jiggled, popped like pebbles spitting out under a car tire, and pulled themselves together. She gathered the pieces with care and headed back to her room.

She stood in the doorway. What was left of Nicole stirred in the fan's breeze and leaked out of the outfit. Penny placed the previously broken clown likenesses lovingly back in their spots. She gathered the clothes, shook Nicole dust out, and placed them back into their place in her closet. Down the hall she retrieved a vacuum and sucked up Nicole dust, then emptied it into an outside garbage can.

We didn't. We eat from you. You sustain and take care of us. We take care of you. You ate her.

"I ate her —" Penny repeated.

We are one.

"What happens when you need to eat next time?"

You will provide.

"And if I don't, then what?"

Die and join us.

Sixteen and senior year were right around the corner. She could move out and live alone. Some part of her really cared for the collection, each and every piece; maybe she even loved it – *really* loved it. They were really one, she knew – many faces, but a single collective. "What would it be like, joining you? Would it be like Nicole?"

Nicole's soul is not ours. Yours. We are one.

"So I would be just a part of you, then? Just one?"

You are like us. You are a collective. We would be two.

A tear slipped down her cheek, but it wasn't for Nicole, or her mother. Penny's heart ached for it – a collective of souls, yet alone. She realized that no matter how much it "ate," it would ever know love or real companionship. This relationship of devotion and nurture was all it knew or could know, unless she joined it.

Penny picked out an outfit and dressed. She put on makeup and perfume. She gathered her clowns and packed them with care into boxes. She labeled the boxes, sending them to her friend Kia in Japan – a like-minded young man she'd met on Facebook. He'd take care of them and her. Penny phoned FEDEX and arranged for the boxes to be picked up. She had them add the cost to her mother's company tab. About that she was relieved and thankful. She carried the boxes one-by-one to the front porch.

"I want to join you," Penny said, "but need to do a couple of things and, if you'll agree, I want to go back to my room."

We agree. We love you.

Her phone buzzed again. She picked it up and read the text from her mother: *I'll be later than planned.* Penny typed: *Nicole went to the mall. I'm staying in and watching one of my Stephen King horror DVDs. We ate pizza.* Her mom replied: *Ok, sounds fine.* Penny set the phone aside. Oddly, she didn't feel the guilt or remorse for her sister as she thought she would. She felt relieved. "What did you mean before when you said *you* instead of *we* ate Nicole?"

Penny changed her mined. She called FEDEX and cancelled the order. Then she took all her clown posters, dolls, and sculptures. Everything out of the packages that she was going to send to Kia and brought them out to the backyard, creating a big colorful pile. She stared at the collage of bright colors, happy faces and realized how much of her life had been devoured by these clowns. They didn't make her happy, only sad. A few tears spilled down her face.

What are you doing? We don't like it out here. It is cold. Bring us back inside to your room. You are one of us now.

"You're cold?" Penny asked. "Okay. I'll warm you up." She took out a match, lit it, and tossed it onto the clown pile, which erupted into a fireball of colors. Soon all the painted smiles went up in smoke.

I always wanted to write a story about gargoyles or demons. In fact, at one point, R.L. Fox and I even outlined a book called INTERVIEW WITH THE DEVIL, but I ended up writing LIQUID DIET & MIDNIGHT SNACK instead.

ALONE WITH A DEMON
by Michael McCarty

1.

The night swallowed the town of Hades, Texas like a coyote devouring a Diamondback in the cold desert dunes. The death rattles shook out the last, faint glows of twilight in the early night sky.

The flashing red and blue lights from Deputy Quinn Navarro's squad car lit up the desert night sky. The law officer was a lank man with a pencil thin moustache, a military buzz haircut, and thick dark eyebrows. He waited for the driver to roll down her window.

"Happy belated birthday Quinn," said fifty-year old lady with cascades of blonde hair with only a faint streak of gray in it. She was trying to sound as cheerful as she could, after the annoyance of being pulled over. The name on her licenses read Gabrielle Abigail Moss, but everybody called her Gabby Abbey or just plain Gabby.

"Thank you, Gabby. But that's D-e-p-u-ty Quinn."

She dismissed his formality. If he'd shone the flashlight at her face, he would've seen that she'd rolled her eyes, too.

"Do you know why I pulled you over?"

"You were really bored?"

"While that may be true, that isn't why I pulled you over." He paused for effect. "I pulled you over because you ran a stop sign."

"Oh," she said surprised, then paused with her head slightly bowed, trying to suppress a giggle. "I will stop twice at the next one."

The deputy tried to hide his grin, but his chuckle escaped. He hadn't heard that one before.

He shone the flashlight into her car and was not surprised that she was wearing only a thin blue nightgown and a silver cross around her neck. He quickly turned it off. "Gabby, it is getting late. You really should go on back home –"

Her first impulse was to argue, but she knew he was right. "Okay, I will."

"And remember the sign the next time."

Gabby honked and waved as she pulled back onto the highway – eyeing her rear-view mirror.

The smile remained on his face as Quinn got back into his cruiser.

2.

In Davenport, Iowa, rays of sunshine filtered in through broken blinds onto the California king-sized bed. Jake Cassidy rolled over, squinted, and mumbled, "So, it begins all over again."

Alone. The solitude was so common these days since Melissa had passed away. The six months felt more like six years. He still wasn't used to waking up without his wife by his side.

The case was settled out of court. For Jake it wasn't about the money. It was about Melissa's parents desire for retribution. Jake's name was added to the plaintiff list of the case as a recommendation from their attorney. Otherwise, if the settlement had not came so swift, he might have continued his career as a clinical professor at Kracken College of Chiropractics.

He needed space, the open road.

With the money, he went to truck-driving school and got his CDL. An old family friend, Bud, hired him without hesitation---so fast, in fact, that he jumped straight into the job driving a rig at Bud Monson's Trucking Company the day after graduation.

He was alone, but the open road was its own kind of therapy.

He should have been used to being alone, but his wife's past stuck firmly to him like a fabric softer sheet with static cling. He remembered how Melissa's her hair always smelled like lilacs and her body was always warm when they snuggled together. It didn't matter the temperature of the room, she was always warm.

Jake sipped on the lukewarm coffee from his mug, the breakfast of champions, and made his way to work. He was going to drop off the truck and take off for a couple of days of R&R, maybe read a Joe McKinney novel and watch some On Demand to get caught up on his series he missed on the road – those were his goals.

After he parked the semi in the garage bay, he climbed out of the rig and started walking when he felt a tap on his shoulder. He turned around to a tall man in greasy overalls, Eddie Monson, the mechanic and son of Bud.

"Bud wants to see you right away," Eddie said, between chewing a wad of gum in his mouth loudly.

"Okay," he said, walking towards Bud Monson Junior's office, the assistant manager of the trucking company.

"No, it is Senior who wants to see ya," Eddie yelled at him.

Jake stopped in his tracks and turned around to look at the mechanic. "I'm not getting fired am I?"

The mechanic shrugged his shoulders. "Doubt it. We are too short handed right now."

"Okay." Jake hesitated then turned around and walked towards Bud Monson Sr.'s office located at the end of the bay. The office was rather small and plastered with photos of naked women; it also needed a good cleaning. The boss' desk was with cluttered with papers and empty energy drink cans. Bud was sitting at the computer when Jake came in. He jabbed at a key and a screen saver popped up, like someone who was just watching porn or hiding bad income figures.

"Shut the door and have a seat," his boss commanded.

Jake did as he was told. "I'm not going to get fired or laid off, am I?"

"Nothing like that," his boss said, dismissing the idea with a wave of his hand. "Just want a little privacy."

"Good," the truck driver said as he wiped away the beads of sweat that were forming on his forehead.

"How long have you been with the company?"

"Six months."

"And you like your job?"

"Yes." He tried to put on the best smile he could muster with such tension in the room.

"Good." The boss tapped his fingers on his desk like he was plucking guitar strings, paused for another moment, and then said, "Meet me in Bay Number Three."

Bud picked up a briefcase and he and Jake walked in silence toward the bay. As they approached, Jake's chest tightened. It was dark and dirty; the skylight was so filthy that only a few beams of light penetrated through the glass.

Bud stood next to a white semi truck with a box cargo that had a bottle of soda in bright letters that read: "Super-Charged Root Beer."

Jake studied the truck for a moment. "Isn't that kind of small for a freight truck?" he asked.

"Very observant. The average freight truck is anywhere between 28-52 feet long. This truck is only 20 feet long."

"That root beer must not be very popular," he said with a grin.

"Not at all. The soda sells millions each year."

"Why such a small truck."

"Because it isn't going to haul root beer. But I'm getting ahead of myself. This truck was specifically made for this delivery."

Jake had a confused looked on his face.

"We're going to make a lot of money with this baby," Bud said, patting the side of the truck.

At that moment, a loud roar came from inside the truck.

"Shut the hell up in there," his boss yelled.

The roar ceased.

"Are you hauling lions?" Jake studied the truck more. "Hey, I don't see any breathing holes for animals."

"Very observant again. But to answer your question, look at the roof."

He studied it for a few moments "It is just a roof."

"You are correct. Just in case a helicopter or a small plane flies over the truck, the pilot won't see a thing. Like I said, this truck was made just for this delivery. But to answer your question, oxygen is being pumped inside the cargo in back," his boss said. "Before we go any further I need you to sign a nondisclosure contract." He opened up the brief case and brought out a clipboard with several pages on it, then handed it to Jake. "I need you to sign page one and page sixty and date them."

Jake skimmed them, signed the papers, and handed the clipboard back. "What is this all about?"

"You were chosen for a great opportunity."

"Chosen?"

"Yes by the people who want and are paying for this delivery." He opened up his briefcase again and brought out a piece of paper. "This is what you make every two weeks, right?"

Jake looked at the figure and nodded.

"Once you drive this vehicle out of this bay, that amount of money will be directly deposited into your account. Once you return the truck back to the bay after you drop off the delivery, you will get the exact amount of money deposited into your account again. All for just two days' work "

Jake let that thought toss about inside his brain. "That is a lot of money for just two days."

"Hell, yeah, it is. And all you have to do is deliver this truck nonstop to Hades, Texas, drop it off at the underground military base that is disguised as Al's Garage, and then drive the truck back here."

"I've never heard of Hades, Texas," the truck driver lied. He tried to wipe all recognition from his face.

"Located near the Inferno Desert. It is about forty miles southwest of San Antonio. Some dozen or so families – all probably related and in no hurry to meet outsiders."

"Okay. So when do I have to make this delivery?"

"By tomorrow night."

"Whoa. That's illegal. When you said two days' work, I thought you were talking two days there and two days back. That would be breaking the 11/14 hour truck regulation. I don't want to lose my license over this."

His boss sighed. "You're talking about the rule that states drivers can't work more than 14 hours in a 24-hour period and can't drive more than 11 hours in a 24-hour period without taking a 10-hour break."

"Yes," Jake said, the realization of the task hitting him like a ton of bricks, money or no. "How the hell can we get around that rule?"

Without missing a beat, his boss said, "The truck logs and the license plate show you were coming from Little Rock, Arkansas."

Jake was speechless.

"Don't looked all surprised. All the other drivers who work here have at least three logs with them and usually only one is the truth." He walked to the back of the truck and unlocked the doors. "Remember you signed that nondisclosure contract."

His bossed opened the doors all the way and climbed inside. Jake followed.

Inside the vehicle was a giant silver cage with a greenish gray gargoyle-like creature with giant wings folded against it's body. The monster had two sharp tiny horns on the top of his head, red glowing eyes, a dark goatee and, when it smiled, jagged teeth. He had hands instead of hooves with sharp claws on each finger.

"What the hell is *that*?"

"You are very close – a demon, a creature from the depths of hell. I have a few other things to tell you. See that window between the cab and the sleeper? It's there so you can check on the demon from time to time. And if it gets out of line, you have permission to use the bullwhip, or cattle prod, which are next to the cage. If that doesn't work, there is also a shotgun. The monster will bring more money alive than dead and the gun is a last resort."

"What are those slits on the side of its neck."

"Gills."

"Like a fish?"

"Hell if I know." His boss curled Jakes hands around the keys. "The last rule's obvious – DON'T TALK TO IT!"

"Why?"

"Evil can be very persuasive. Remember in the Bible, a demon deceived Eve to make Adam eat the apple and look how all that turned out."

Jake was going to correct his boss and tell him that it wasn't a demon, but the Devil himself and both Adam and Eve ate the forbidden fruit, then decided otherwise.

"One last thing. That cage is made out silver and very expensive. Try not to damage it."

"Silver. Why?"

His boss wriggled his fingers. "Maybe it's magical. Maybe it works like a silver bullet on a werewolf. Maybe the creature is allergic to it. Hell if I know. Just stay alert. There will be a first class ticket at the airport for you to fly back after you make the delivery. And you'll get the rest of the money when you're back."

3.

When Jake drove the Super-Charged Root Beer truck onto I-80 heading out of Davenport, he pulled the semi over to the side of the road and put on the airbrakes, releasing a whoosh sound. He took his cell phone out of his pocket and did a search for his bank account, punched in a series of numbers and the bank account suddenly had grown with a direct deposit from his employer.

"You think that's a lot of money? That is just chump change."

Jake looked around to see who was talking to him. There was nobody else in his cab. Then he looked through the sliding window in back; it was the demon.

"A four-zero deposit is nothing compared to the seven-zero deposit your employer just received," the demon said.

"Seven zeros?"

"And they will get another seven zeros after you drop me off. Like I said, chump change."

"Hey, I'm not supposed to talk to you."

"You do everything you're told? If your boss, after cashing in that seven zero check, told you to jump off a bridge, would you?"

"No."

"Exactly."

At that moment, the demon unfolded his wings and pulled out a cigar box he kept hidden there. He took out a cigar, stuck it in his mouth. Then he snapped his fingers and his index finger started to burn. He raised the burning finger to the cigar and lit it, blew out the flame and started puffing smoke.

"This is a smoke free truck."

"Christ-on-a-stick," the demon said. "I'm caged like some kind of an animal and you're worried that I'm smoking. It's a Cuban cigar and they're hard to get. Can't you at least let me enjoy it? I won't light anymore."

"But what about the oxygen being pumped in."

The demon dismissed the hazard with a wave of his clawed fingers.

"I really don't have time to chat with you —" Jake wasn't sure what to call him, "Mr. Demon. I'm on a tight deadline."

"Beat the clock. Race the devil. Time will always win. It's a lost cause. Don't worry about such mundane things. I've got that covered. See that Volkswagen in your mirror. Keep watching it."

Jake looked in his side mirror and sure enough – there was a red Volkswagen Beetle in the distance. He looked at it. In about a minute it should have passed the truck. He kept looking at it – the vehicle didn't move.

"Did that car break down?"

"Nope. Guess again."

"You froze that car. How did you do that?"

"I didn't freeze the Beetle. I just slowed it down. I slow down time. Time right now is going at a lot slower pace; one hour will equal about one minute in real time. Fairly easy to do for us demons. Lighting my cigar was a bit harder." He took another puff from his cigar and blew out a perfect smoke ring.

"What's so important to talk about, that you had to slow time?"

"I rarely get to talk with a human. You're quite perplexing to me. I have some questions."

"Okay. Fire away."

"What's up with straws?"

"Are you serious?"

"I can be." The demon paused, then grinned.

"Is everything a game to you?"

"It can be."

"I'm not playing games with an Imp."

"Alright. Alright. Okay. I'll be serious." The demon scratched his goatee, then asked, "Why do they call you Jake The Snake?"

Jake laughed. "I haven't heard that name in a long time. I grew up in Southern Missouri. When I was in grade school. I'd pick up any snake for a dollar."

"Rattlers?"

"Yes sir, a few."

"Were you stupid, brave, or greedy."

"Probably all three," Jake paused for a moment.

"You were born and raised in Missouri. How did you end up in Iowa?"

"I came up here to go to Kracken College of Chiropractics, met Melissa there and eventually ended up teaching classes." Just saying his wife's name again hurt. Just like pulling off an old scab, it created a new wound.

There was a moment of silence.

Jake cleared his throat and said "I have a question for you. Why do you have gills on the sides of your neck?"

"It's for extra breathing. Being as hot as hell in Hell you need to breathe more and the gills help with that."

"How did you get captured?"

The demon sighed. "I'd rather not talk about that or the fact when you drop me off to Al's Garage – which is really underground military base – the scientists there will just slice and dice me."

"Okay. So what were you doing on Earth in the first place?"

"That's an easy one. Spying on humans. There's a lot of demons sent to Earth to spy."

The demon shifted his weight in the cage to get more comfortable. "Wanna learn a magic trick? Let me go and your bosss will have seven zeros disappear like that," the demon snapped his fingers.

"And I'd lose my job just as fast. I'm not foolish enough to let a demon loose onto Earth."

"You can't blame a demon for trying," he said with a sinister smile.

"Look, I really just want to get this job behind me. It's going to be a long drive."

"I can speed up time, so it only takes a few minutes to get to Hades, Texas."

"You can do that?"

"Slow down time, speed it up. All very easy to do."

"You'd do that for me?"

"I'm a demon of my word. But let's talk a little longer."

"Okay."

"I asked the last couple of questions. Now, it is your turn."

"What is Hell like? Have you ever been to Heaven?"

"Demons aren't allowed in Heaven."

"So what is Hell like?"

For the first time, the demon was quiet in thought. "It is hard to describe because it is more abstract than what is here, more darkly surreal."

"Give it your best shot."

"Dark, hot, and overcrowded like the deepest darkest place in your nightmares. When you get there you wake up screaming."

"What happens when you first get to Hell?" Jake asked.

"You lose your face, name, identity, and are only left with your memories."

"Memories?"

"The most dark and painful ones."

"What do you mean, lose your face?"

"Your face melts away until you are left with only your skull."

"I don't want to talk about Hell anymore."

4.

Deputy Quinn Navarro stepped out of his squad car and approached the Saturn in front of him. He was wearing his uniform, complete with a badge, a Smith & Wesson M&P .45 caliber automatic pistol in his holster, and forty-five dollars in bills in his wallet.

The deputy couldn't shake the feeling of déjà vu, since he found himself in the same place where he'd pulled Gabby Abbey over the night before.

Gabby had rolled her window down again and said, "My favorite Law Dog."

"Law Dog?"

"It means policeman. I heard the term on a TV show."

"Oh. Do you know why I pulled you over?"

"You are looking for a date?"

Quinn almost smiled. "No Gabby. You ran the same stop sign as last night."

"I stopped."

"It was more of a slow and go. You didn't come to a complete stop. You could've run over a critter or something."

"If I hit a coyote, big deal. They just attack innocent rabbits out here anyway."

"You promised me last night you'd stop twice at the next stop sign."

"Sorry about that. I have a lot on my mind."

He turned on his flashlight and pointed it into the car. Gabby wore the same nightgown and the same big sliver cross around her neck as the night before when he'd stopped her.

"If you keep that flashlight on me any longer, you're going to have to give me a dollar for putting on a show."

"May I ask what you're doing driving the Inferno Desert this hour in your night clothes?"

"You may ask, but I don't have to answer."

"Come on Gabby."

She looked in the rearview mirror. The flashing red and blue lights made her hair look less than flattering. "I couldn't sleep."

"Oh."

"The universe keeps me awake at night."

"Thinking about Dale?"

Hearing the name of her deceased husband broke her heart yet again. "Yes," she could barely utter.

"Dale was a decent, hardworking guy who always looked out for others. He recommended me for this job, which I am eternally grateful for."

"Thanks for the kind words," she said. "Do you know what his last words were?"

"No, Gabby? What were they?"

"'Fill my heart with love and stone.'" She sighed. "What does that mean?"

"I have no idea," the deputy replied. "He was in a lot of pain. People say all kinds of things when they're in terrible pain."

She let the idea tumble around in her head for a few moments. "That does make sense."

The deputy swallowed the lump in his throat. "Gabby, go home. Drink some warm milk. That might help you sleep."

"Those who think there's some kind of time limit for grieving, have never lost a large part of their heart. You know what I mean?"

"Yes, I do." The deputy said. He paused, lowering the flashlight. "Please, go home. Try to get some sleep."

She nodded. "Okay." She started up her car and drove into the dark dessert.

5.

"We should be leaving," Jake said.

"Just one more question," the demon said.

"Okay."

"Why do you carry a pack of gum, when you don't really chew gum?"

"I chew-up a piece up gum and when I go to a truck stop for the night, I put the chewed gum on my front tire, so the Lot Lizards let me sleep."

"Lot Lizards?"

"Hookers, whores, ladies of the evening, or whatever you want to call them. When they're done servicing you, they put a piece of chewed gum on your tire, so other Lot Lizards will leave you alone. Sort of like the 'Do Not Disturb' sign at a hotel."

"So, why did you lie to your boss about Hades, Texas?"

"Okay, so I lied. My ex-girlfriend Gabby Abbey lives there. I've been following her on Facebook. I didn't want to tell my boss about it because it seems so cyber stalking-ish."

"The girlfriend you dated before meeting your wife, who is now a widow?"

"Yeah," he said with a sheepish expression on his face.

"Are you going to see her after you drop me off to get sliced and diced?"

"No, no, I can't."

The Demon gave him a stern look. "You can't or you won't? The other thing I learned about humans is their lives are way too short."

"I don't want to talk about this anymore. You promised me you'd speed up time. You gave me your word. Let's do it, then."

"Start up the truck, shift into drive, and hold onto the steering wheel for dear life. You're in for a rough ride."

Jake started up the truck, shifted into drive, put it into high gear, and was going down the road at sixty-five miles per hour. All of a sudden, everything got dark and blurry. It was like the time he rode Space Mountain at the Disney amusement park except at rocket-speed, a lot more frightening and disorienting. It was as if he'd just taken drugs and was hallucinating on a bad trip. Then the truck suddenly stopped. He was in the dark desert next to a lit two-story house.

A lady in her early fifties came running out of the house with a loaded shotgun in her hands. She wore a white terry cloth robe and pink cowboy boots; she had cucumber cream all over her face and a white bath towel wrapped around her head like a turban. It had been over twenty years since he saw her last, but he immediately knew that it was Gabby Abbey.

"You'd better have a damn good reason for parking your rig in front of my house or I'm going to fill you and your truck with lead," the lady said, running to the side of the truck. She saw the driver was Jake.

"Jake? Jake Cassidy?"

Jake stepped out of the truck. "Gabby. You still remember me."

"How could I ever forget?"

They hugged each other tightly.

"Let's go inside."

6.

The demon stuck one sharp claw in the door lock and picked it with ease, but when he touched it his flesh seared and smoked. He recoiled, recovered, and gave the door a quick, hard shove; it swung open and he stepped out. Humans, he'd learned, were as cruel or crueler than demons in Hell. Who knew? As he opened the rear doors, the hot, humid Texas night air washed over him. It felt a bit like home in a wetter, less fiery sort of way. He smiled his toothy grin, spread his wings, and flew into the dark night.

7.

Jake sat on the love seat, drinking his red wine. "Can you get arrested for killing time?" he asked, laughing.

"Had to do hard time for killing it," she quipped back.

"Don't do the crime, if you don't have the time."

"How do you like working as a truck driver?" Gabby asked.

"It's okay," Jake replied. "You know what my dad used to say about work?"

"No."

"He'd say, '"There was work before I was born. And there will be work after I die.'"

"Your dad was a wise man."

"Yes he was," he said with a sigh. "I'm sorry I missed the funeral of your husband."

"Dale wouldn't let me go to that funeral or your wife's."

"Because they're so far away? Texas to Iowa?"

"That. And he knew I always had the hots for you. Still do."

Gabby sat on the loveseat with Jake. She started to unbutton his shirt.

"What are you doing?" he asked.

"Trying to get a better view of your heart," she replied with a giggle. She ran her finger across his chest.

"So, can you see my heart?"

"Of course not, I don't have x-ray vision. But I can listen to it." She put her head softly against his chest.

"What is my ticker saying?"

"Your heartbeat sounds like bang boom, bang boom, bang boom."

"I wonder what 'bang boom' means?"

"It means you want to take me up to my bedroom. I haven't slept with anyone since Dale passed away, but tonight seems right."

The glasses of wine were put down and soon they went into each other's arms.

8.

The demon was flying in place above the second floor bedroom window. He cocked his head to peek inside. He saw two bodies merging as one. The bed bounced and squeaked with their efforts, the headboard tapping out the rhythm.

"The way humans mate is so mundane compared to how we do it in hell," he said to himself. He flew towards the big orange moon, low on the horizon and smiled. It was an impish grin.

9.

Larry Higgins, the owner of Hades Cafe had his shotgun in one hand and his bottle of whiskey in the other with his dirty apron wrapped around his waist. A commotion by the trashcans in the backyard drew him out to the backyard. If it was some raccoons or possums messing in the trash cans they'd soon meet their maker.

Another trashcan was knocked over.

"Die Possum," he said, as he aimed the shotgun towards the cans. No possum or coon crawled out.

The noise sounded louder. Larry was wondered if it might be a stray dog or some wild boar tearing up his trash, but instead, it was a demon.

"Surprise!" said the demon as he swooped onto the café owner and sunk his sharp claws into Larry's shoulders and neck. The pain was unbearable. He dropped his shotgun.

As the café owner raised his arms to fend off the attacker, the demon twisted his grip on Larry's neck, decapitating him. His head flew through the air like a baseball smacked by a pro, spraying a blood trail as it turned over and over, until it hit the ground bouncing then rolling, slowing, and coming to a rocking stop, his open eyes looking toward the heavens.

"Well, I guess I lost that toss. Looks like heads," the demon said.

The demon extended its wings and dragged Larry's headless corpse straight up into the air. When he reached sufficient height, he released his prized. After the dead body splattered hitting the ground, he chuckled and yelled, "Tails!" then flew even higher into the clouds.

10.

"It's not a wham-bam-thank-you-dead ma'am," Jake said, buttoning his shirt as he walked out from the porch towards his truck.

"Okay, just call it, 'screw and run' then."

"It's not that either," he stopped, turned around and hugged her. "I will be back after I delivery this truck. Then I can stay with you the rest of the weekend."

She scrunched her face up. "Promise?"

"Of course," he said hugging her tightly. I'll be back shortly after —" He stopped in mid sentence when he saw the back of his truck was open. Jake ran to the open doors and saw the cage doors were open too. "It escaped."

"What escaped?"

"I can't tell you because I signed a non-disclosure contract."

They both looked at each other with an uncomfortable silence.

"Screw it – at this point I don't care. A monster. A winged demon from hell —"

11.

Jake finished telling all about the demon and the journey from Iowa to the Lone Star State and said, "Well?" What do you think?"

Gabby was about to answer when they were interrupted by the sound of something smashing onto the barn roof and sliding off onto something behind barn, landing with a bone-breaking crunch-splat.

"What was that Jake?"

"Back to the truck." They both crept in silence, back to Jake's truck.

Jake handed Gabby the flashlight."

"Shhhh. Quiet!" Jake paused, realizing she knew the property not him. "You should lead, but I'll be right behind you. I promise."

Gabby hesitated and stopped a few times, as she led the way with the flashlight, to the back of the barn.

Motionless. There it was. Tangled up in the engine bay of a neglected Chevy pick-up – Larry's headless body mixed red, with 10-40 weight splatter on the ground.

"Air-delivery assholes – No charge," quipped the imp from the ridge of the barn with a haunting glee.

As if in a show of dominance, or perhaps a bit of devilish admiration, the creature from Hell swooped in a power-dive fly by inches from their faces. It was so fast, Jake and Gabby struggled to focus on it as it faded into the dark with one hand raised and one finger rolled out.

12.

Deputy Quinn had finished up all the paperwork for the night and locked up the back door to the Hades Police Department. He was walking to his car in the parking lot when he felt sharp claws sink into his shoulder. The pain raced through his entire body and before he could scream, he was lifted high into the air on the dark horizon.

13.

They stood beside the barn for several minutes. Gabby finally broke the silence. "I have an idea. You told me that silver hurts the demon, right?"

"Yeah."

"If we melt down some silver and put it on the tips of my arrows, I can shoot the demon with my bow. Remember, I was really good in archery in college. I even won a few torments."

"Do you have any silver to melt?"

"Yes. A silver cross. But it was a gift from my late husband." She paused. "Dale loved this town and would do anything to protect it, including melting this cross."

14.

Gabby laid the silver cross on the flat stone in the crucible of fire and clay. It took several minutes, but eventually the metal on the cross started to bubble and began to melt. They poured the melted silver onto the tips of seven arrows. She didn't wait for the arrowheads to cool. She grabbed them and the bow and headed outside with Jake in tow to the barn.

"I'm going to hide in that gully," she pointed near the barn. "I want you to distract him so I can get a good aim."

"How am I going to distract him?"

"I have no idea."

She hid in the gully with her bow and silver-tipped arrows; he stood by the barn.

The winged demon carrying deputy Quinn descended near the barn doors.

Jake stepped out into the opening, rattling his keys. "Demon," he said still shaking the keys. "Playtime's over. Time to go back inside your cage."

"Who's going to make me?" said the creature from Hell with a laugh.

"Me," Gabby said, springing up out of the gully, pulling the arrow back from the bow and releasing it. The arrow flew with a whizzing sound, piercing through both wings of the demon as it arced and disappeared. He dropped from the sky and had a rough landing near the barn.

The monster cried out in pain, dropping the law officer to the ground as it fell.

Quinn tried to stand up, but was in too much pain to do so. "I think the fall broke my leg," he cried out.

Gabby grabbed another arrow, but this time Jake took it from her hands and ran the arrowhead into the creature's chest bending the tip, not penetrating its armor.

"You said you were a demon of your word?"

"Yeah."

"You promise to leave this town and never return."

"Yeah."

Jake thought about it for a moment. "Have you ever kept your word?"

"No."

At that moment the demon lunged at Jake. He jumped aside and the creature crashed against a barrel and lost its balance.

Jake took out a flask from his back pocket and splashed it onto the demon's face.

The demon cried out a gargling hiss of agony under the crackling hiss of the liquid burning his face. The monster cried out an unholy curse as it

198

tried to wipe away the holy fluid.

Jake pointed the arrow's silver tip about an inch from the demon's left eye. "You lost a wing. Should I take an eye too?"

"NO! NO! NO!"

"I'll let you live, but you must go back to Hell where you came from. "

The two peered deep into each-others eyes in a stand-off that seemed endless.

"I will go – for now..." The demon stood and limped its way toward the highway and Hell, maybe even the highway to Hell. Gabby and Jake hear it mumble, "Let the games begin."

15.

The events over the next couple of weeks happened at light speed. Jake called his employer telling him that he had no choice but to release the demon. His boss fired him and even threatened to sue, until he found out that Jake also threatened to release the bogus records to the DOT and report the story to the media and social media. The law suit was dropped, but Jake was still out of a job.

Jake drove the truck back to his employer, but took a passenger with him – Gabby. After dropping off the truck and getting some of his belongings from home, he returned to Hades, Texas with her. Gabby and Jake who were once alone were now together. They drove into town as a big orange sun began to rise over the horizon.

ABOUT THE AUTHORS:

MICHAEL McCARTY:

Michael McCarty has been a professional writer since 1983, and the author of over forty books of fiction and nonfiction, including *I Kissed A Ghoul, A Little Help From My Fiends, Dark Duets, Liquid Diet & Midnight Snack, Monster Behind The Wheel* (co-written with Mark McLaughlin), *Dracula Transformed and Other Bloodthirsty Tales* (also with Mark McLaughlin), *Lost Girl Of The Lake* (with Joe McKinney), the vampire *Bloodless* series: *Bloodless, Bloodlust* and *Bloodline* (co-written with Jody LaGreca). He is a five-time Bram Stoker Finalist and in 2008 won the David R. Collins' Literary Achievement Award from the Midwest Writing Center.

He is also the author of the mega book of interviews *Modern Mythmakers: 35 Interviews With Horror And Science Fiction Writers And Filmmakers* which features interviews with Ray Bradbury, Dean Koontz, John Carpenter, Richard Matheson, Elvria, Linnea Quigley, John Saul, Joe McKinney, and many more.

Michael McCarty lives in Rock Island, Illinois with his wife Cindy and pet rabbit Latte.

Michael McCarty is on Twitter as michaelmccarty6.

His blog site is at: http://monstermikeyaauthor.wordpress.com

Facebook! Like him on his official page:

http://www.facebook.com/michaelmccarty.horror.

Or snail mail him at:

Michael McCarty

Fan Mail

P.O. Box 4441

Rock Island, IL 61204-4441

JOE McKINNEY:

Joe McKinney has his feet in several different worlds. In his day job he has worked as a patrol officer for the San Antonio Police Department, a DWI Enforcement officer, a disaster mitigation specialist, a homicide detective, the director of the City of San Antonio's 911 Call Center, and a patrol supervisor. He played college baseball for Trinity University, where he graduated with a Bachelor's Degree in American History, and went on to earn a Master's Degree in English Literature from the University of Texas at San Antonio. He was the manager of a Barnes & Noble for a while, where he indulged a lifelong obsession with books.

He published his first novel, *Dead City,* in 2006, a book that has since been recognized as a seminal work in the zombie genre. Since then, he has gone on to win two Bram Stoker Awards and expanded his oeuvre to cover everything from true crime and writings on police procedure to science fiction to cooking to Texas history. The author of more than twenty books, he is a frequent guest at horror and mystery conventions. Joe and his wife Tina have two lovely daughters and make their home in a little town just outside of San Antonio, where he pursues his passion for cooking and makes what some consider to be the finest batch of chili in Texas. You can keep up with all of Joe's latest releases by friending him on Facebook.

MARK McLAUGHLIN:

Mark McLaughlin's latest trade paperback releases are the story collections; *Best Little Witch-House In Arkham, Beach Blanket Zombie* and *Hideous Faces, Beautiful Skulls.* He also is the co-author of the horror collection, *Dracula Transformed & Other Bloodthirsty Tales* (with Michael McCarty) and the collaborative horror novel, *Monster Behind The Wheel* (also with Michael McCarty).

Mark's latest digital releases are the Kindle fiction collections, *Magic Cannot Die, The Creature In The Waxworks* (Co-Written With Michael Sheehan, Jr.), *The Relic In The Egyptian Gallery* (Co-Written With Michael Sheehan, Jr.), *Shoggoth Apocalypse* (Co-Written With Michael Sheehan, Jr.), *The Blasphemy In The Canopic Jar* (Co-Written With Michael Sheehan, Jr.), *The Horror In The Water Tower* (Co-Written With Michael Sheehan, Jr.),

Foreign Tongue; Drunk On The Wine That Pours From My Wicked Eyes And The Abominations Of Nephren-Ka (Co-Written With Michael Sheehan, Jr.).

Mark's fiction, nonfiction, and poetry have appeared in more than 1,000 magazines, newspapers, websites, and anthologies, including *Dark Fusions: Where Monsters Lurk!, Galaxy, Living Dead 2, Writer's Digest, Cemetery Dance, Midnight Premiere, Dark Arts,* and two volumes of *Year's Best Horror Stories* (DAW Books).

Mark is the coauthor, with Rain Graves and David Niall Wilson, of *The Gossamer Eye*, which won the 2002 Bram Stoker Award for Superior Achievement in Poetry.

C.L. SHERWOOD

C.L. Sherwood hails from Deep East Texas and leads a triple life — one as an educator, teaching English and literature to the world's next generation of college goers and future writers, another as a freelance writer and editor, and lastly as a darkly and somewhat depraved horror writer whose supernatural short stories have appeared in publications such as *Eldritch Tales* and *Mangled Matters* online.

Michael McCarty is the author of over 40 books including *Modern Mythmakers, Dark Duets, A Little Help From My Fiends, I Kissed A Ghoul* and *Apocalypse America!* (co-written with Mark McLaughlin). He is also a 5 Time Bram Stoker Finalist and lives in Rock Island, Illinois with his wife and pet rabbit Latte.